ACCOLADES FOR THE REX G[...]

"Challinor will keep most readers gu[...] suspicion and clues that point in one direction, then ano[...]"

—*Alfred Hitchcock Mystery Magazine*

"Look out, Hercule Poirot; Rex Graves will give you a run for your money."   —OnceUponARomance.net

"Authors are sometimes compared to Dame Agatha but few of their books have those characteristics and—more important—the overall feel of hers. *Christmas is Murder* does."

—CozyLibrary.com

"An engaging whodunit … [t]he story effortlessly combines elements of a classic country house mystery with an Agatha Christie-style denouement to great effect."   —MysteriousReviews.com

"Ms. Challinor was educated in Scotland and England, which explains how she writes so convincingly of both her setting and her characters."   —*Florida Weekly*

"Who wouldn't take a case in the land of sun, blue water, and delightful breeze …? There are lots of suspects, red herrings, and plot twists in this traditional mystery in a unique setting."

—*Kaw Valley Senior Monthly* (Kansas)

"A great start to a new series that is sure to become a modern favorite traditional English cozy series. 4 stars."

—TheMysteryReader.com

PHI BETA MURDER

A Rex Graves Mystery

PHI BETA MURDER

C.S. Challinor

MIDNIGHT INK
WOODBURY, MINNESOTA

First Edition
First Printing, 2010

Book design and format by Donna Burch
Cover design by Gavin Dayton Duffy
Editing by Connie Hill

Midnight Ink, an imprint of Llewellyn Publications

Library of Congress Cataloging-in-Publication Data (Pending).
ISBN: 978-0-7387-1890-3

This is a work of fiction. Names, characters, places, and incidents are either the product of the author's imagination or are used fictitiously, and any resemblance to actual persons, living or dead, business establishments, events, or locales is entirely coincidental.

Midnight Ink
Llewellyn Publications
2143 Wooddale Drive, Dept. 978-0-7387-1890-3
Woodbury, MN 55125-2989 USA
www.midnightinkbooks.com

Printed in the United States of America

CAST OF CHARACTERS

Rex Graves—Scottish Barrister, QC, and part-time sleuth

Moira Wilcox—Rex's ardent ex-flame back from Iraq

Mrs. Graves—Rex's aging but spry mother who lives in Edinburgh

Campbell Graves—Rex's son, sophomore at Hilliard University in Jacksonville, Florida

Helen d'Arcy—Rex's current love interest

Dixon Clark—resident assistant found dead in his dorm room

Kris Florek—victim's girlfriend attending the School of Nursing

Justin Paul—clean-cut jock "Greek" of Phi Beta Kappa, a less than squeaky clean fraternity

Andy Palmer—bookworm who enjoys chemistry experiments

"Red" Simmons—engineer student from Colorado, as handy with a rope as a drum kit

Mike Ricardi—Colts fan and fan of Kris Florek, the deceased's girlfriend

"Klepto" Clapham—psychology major with kleptomanic tendencies

R.J. Wylie—expelled student who had everything going for him

Dominic Jean-Baptiste—sultry lead singer-guitarist in Dirty Laundry, a university band

Keith and Katherine Clark—Dixon's grieving parents from Nantucket

Melodie Clark—victim's dead-gorgeous sister

Dr. Binkley—Dean of Students at Hilliard University

Astra Knowles—garrulous School Registrar with her own agenda

Al Cormack—hot-headed mathematics professor

Bethany Johnson—bombshell assistant marine science professor

Becky Ward—on-campus nurse practitioner

Luella Shaw—Klepto's twice-divorced partner

Wayne Price—unsavory police informant

ONE

FROM BLACKFORD HILL, THE volcanic formation of Arthur's Seat resembled a pair of buttocks. People with a more sophisticated imagination likened the shape to a sleeping lion, but Rex thought Arthur's Seat was aptly named. He enjoyed coming up here to clear his head, especially after a heavy week in court or when he had a problem to mull over, as now. For a minute or two, he pondered the troubling phone call from his son, but it was futile to try and read behind what Campbell had said. It would just have to wait until he got to the States.

Yellow-flowered gorse carpeted the grassy slopes on the way up to the top of the lava rock summit. From this vantage point the skyline of the Royal Mile—Edinburgh Castle, the Highland Tolbooth, the hollow-crowned tower of St. Giles' Cathedral—stood out in crystalline purity, reassuring landmarks that had withstood the test of time and which lent Rex a perspective on the vagaries of life. He had brought Helen up here at Christmas, though the view had not been as spectacular then as on this fresh and sunny spring day.

The sky was so clear he could see, quite distinctly, the road and railway bridges spanning the Firth of Forth, and the Pentland Hills to the south. Feeling warm after his climb, he decided to remove his sweater. Then, seated on a knoll, he watched the swans glide across the reflective blue surface of the loch below and thought of Helen and their time together.

Dreary rain had bleakened the gray stone of the grandiose buildings on Princes Street as they sheltered beneath his brolly, window-shopping at the elegant department stores. Her stay at the house in Morningside had been a hoot (to quote Helen). Separate bedrooms, of course—his mother had even put her on a separate floor for good measure. On the occasions Mrs. Graves had left to attend a charity function and the housekeeper was out shopping, they had managed a few furtive assignations in his room, reminding him nostalgically of his teenage years when he would sneak a girl up the fire escape. Now that he was in his late forties, such subterfuges seemed ridiculous, albeit necessary in view of his mother's strict Presbyterian ways.

Brushing the grass from the seat of his corduroys, he began his descent down the hill. He had worked up an appetite and was wondering what Miss Bird might have prepared for tea when he caught sight of a tiny, dark-haired figure wrapped in a shawl, waving to him from half way down the path. It couldn't be … And yet, upon their approaching one another, he saw that it was indeed Moira, whom he had not seen in at least eighteen months.

"How did you know I'd be here?" he demanded, suspecting the housekeeper of divulging his whereabouts. That morning at breakfast he had mentioned he would be going up Arthur's Seat. "Be sure to take yer sweater," Miss Bird had warned. "It can get windy up there." An old joke that had reduced him to giggles when he was a lad ...

"We used to climb up here all the time," Moira reminded him. "I spotted you from the Crags."

"Sometimes I walk to Blackford Hill or to the Botanic Garden," he said crossly.

"On a fine day you'd go up here for the view."

Admittedly, she knew him well. They had dated for over two years before she went off to Iraq.

"When did you get back?" he asked.

"Last week."

"Did you bring your Australian boyfriend?" It still irked Rex that she had dumped him following months of silence when he didn't know what might have befallen her, and all the while she'd been seeing this Aussie!

"Don't be daft. I wouldna be chasing you up this hill if he were with me."

"What happened to him?"

All Rex knew was that he was a photographer for Sydney News who had rescued Moira from a pile of rubble after a bombing at a Baghdad market. That and the fact he had blue eyes, a detail she had thought fit to mention in her Dear John letter.

"He went back to Australia," she told him.

"Why did you not go with him?"

Her brown eyes avoided his for a moment. "He's married."

"Ah, I see." Rex refrained from asking if she had known that about him when they first became involved. "Listen, Moira. I have to get home to pack. I'm flying to Florida tomorrow to see Campbell. He seems down about something."

Her sharp features expressed shock and disappointment. "I only just got back."

"Well, I didn't know you were coming back. And, anyway, it wouldna've made a difference."

"What do you mean?"

Sticking his hands in the pockets of his pants, he fingered through the loose change. "I'm seeing someone else."

"Who is she?"

"You don't know her."

"And how long has this been going on?"

That was a difficult question to answer. He had only been intimate with Helen since the summer, after he received the farewell note from Moira, but he had kept in contact with her since he had met her while solving his first case.

"Fifteen months," he informed Moira. "I told her about you and said there could never be more than a friendship between us while I was seeing you. Though technically I wasna seeing you since you were miles away in Iraq." His Scots accent intensified as always when he was stressed.

"You don't need to sound so het up about it. It was my work that kept me there."

"It was always about your work, Moira. Aye, I know," Rex said, warding off her objections with a grandiose wave. "It's right commendable what you've been doing for the Iraqi civilians and what have you. I respected that and I was prepared to wait. It's you who veered from the path—not I." He didn't even know why he was bothering to have this conversation. It was over between them.

"You have no idea what it's like out there!"

"I don't," Rex conceded. "Look, let's drop it." He stood aside to allow a group of walkers to pass on the slope.

"I made a mistake and I came to tell you I'm sorry!"

"Apology accepted. Take care of yourself, Moira." Turning abruptly, he continued down the path.

She grabbed his arm. "Ye canna jist leave," she pleaded. "We need to talk!"

"There's nothing more to say."

"Are you in love with her then?"

Rex looked upon Moira's anxious face. He hated emotional scenes. "Aye, I suppose so."

A shrewd gleam of triumph lit her eyes. "You don't sound so sure."

He sighed in exasperation. "I don't know what being in love is supposed to feel like at my age." Yet he felt all the right things for Helen: affection, desire, respect—all the necessary ingredients for love once they spent more time together. As it was, he lived in Scotland and she in north central England.

"Rex," Moira said, reaching for his sleeve again.

"Goodbye, Moira."

He strode off down the hill, confident she would never be able to catch up with him, even in her sensible shoes. He blamed her for upsetting his peaceful afternoon. He had wanted to get his thoughts in order before his trip to Florida, and she had thrown them in turmoil. He even found himself wishing she had stayed in Iraq or else emigrated to Australia. He didn't need this extra complication in his life.

TWO

REX HAD NOT LIKED leaving Moira in a state, but hadn't known what else to do, since he needed to get back home to pack and leave last-minute instructions for his law clerk. That done, he sat down to tea in the parlor.

His mother prided herself on serving the best afternoon tea in Morningside, the tiered cake tray arranged with drop scones prepared by Miss Bird and eaten off gold-rimmed Royal Doulton side plates, the dainty repast conducted with as much ritual as a Japanese tea ceremony.

At Christmas, Helen had had the fortuitous intuition to inquire about the lace doilies on the table, thus ingratiating herself with his mother forever. "Such delicate crochet work. Wherever did you find them?"

"My dear, I made them myself! Likewise the headrest covers on the armchairs. I must give ye a set to take home wi' ye."

Helen had recovered quickly. "That would be lovely, Mrs. Graves, but only if you can spare them. They are truly exquisite."

"Mother can always make some more," Rex assured her.

"Get away wi' ye! They don't grow on trees." Mrs. Graves turned to Helen. "Men have nary an appreciation for the finer things. If it weren't for women, they'd still be living in caves!"

Rex felt this was a gross exaggeration, but confined himself to a patient smile, delighted that the two women were getting on so well.

"I do like your mother," Helen had approved when they found themselves alone. "She's such a grand old lady. Do you think she likes me?"

"You have completely won her over, lass. What are you going to do with the lace doilies?"

"I haven't a clue," Helen admitted, and they had both laughed.

Just as important, Helen got on famously with his son Campbell, who had made a few appearances at the house over the holidays when he wasn't busy catching up with old school friends. She seemed amazingly informed about contemporary music, probably because she worked with teenagers—and had asked Campbell about American groups with names you wouldn't dream of giving a pet hamster.

"Don't forget to take Campbell the sweater I knitted him," his mother said, interrupting his reverie as she poured tea from a fine china pot.

Even in her mid-eighties, her features were still delicate, her figure as graceful as a girl's, although her once red-gold hair had faded to pure white. Her hands retained their dexterity, her green eyes their sharp vision, and she had been able to pursue her needlework and Bible-reading all these years without the aid of spectacles.

"Mother, it's 80 degrees in Florida. Campbell will no be needing a sweater."

"Best he have it just in case. The weather is unpredictable. Remember the flooding they had in England last year and the heat wave in Europe?"

"All right, Mother." Pointless to argue with her, even though he felt certain his son would never wear the tangerine sweater, which even Rex knew was all wrong for his coloring. It would merely be a waste of space in his suitcase.

"There could be another Ice Age over there, for all we know," his mother insisted.

Scenes of destruction from *The Day After Tomorrow* filed through Rex's mind. "Unlikely that would happen in the three years Campbell has left at college," he reasoned.

"I do wish the lad had stayed home. It seems you're always hopping on a plane these days. Now I have to worry about terrorist hijackings, metal fatigue, and the prepackaged food they serve on board."

"You worry too much, Mother."

His father had been killed by a drunk driver, which had put her faith in all things severely to the test.

"It's the phone for ye," the old housekeeper informed him, shuffling into the parlor and giving Rex a meaningful look.

He sighed. It was probably Moira. She had called several times already, leaving frantic messages on his cell phone. "Please take a message, Miss Bird."

"It's Moira," the housekeeper grudgingly confirmed, her eyes sliding to Mrs. Graves.

Rex guessed Moira had not wanted his mother to find out she was calling and had told Miss Bird not to say anything. His mother had been very put out when she discovered Moira had left him for another man.

"Moira Wilcox?" she asked, astounded. "Is she back from Iraq then?"

"Aye, she followed me to Arthur's Seat."

"What shall I tell her?" the housekeeper asked. Miss Bird was a timorous woman and Moira not one to be easily put off.

With an aggravated sigh, Rex threw his napkin aside and rose from the table. In the hall, he picked up the receiver. "Rex here."

"Can we talk?"

"There really is no point, Moira."

"There's every point! You don't understand."

He hated it when women said that. It usually meant, "You are failing to see things from my point of view."

"When are you returning from Florida?"

"In a week," Rex said evasively.

"Can we get together then?"

"Moira... Please don't call me again." He hung up and strode back to the parlor.

"That was a short call," his mother remarked as Miss Bird refilled his tea cup.

"I did not want to take it in the first place." He looked with reproach at the housekeeper, who shrugged her wiry shoulders.

"Well, I dare say you're right," his mother conceded. "But if Moira comes back to the Charitable Ladies of Morningside, it could make things right awkward. And I hope she's not planning on rejoining the bridge club."

Wishing to drop the subject, Rex picked up the crisply folded newspaper on the table. Sometimes it got a bit wearing living under the same roof as two old women. Fortunately he had a private suite upstairs. All his needs were met, from the provision of meals to the ironing of his shirts. Most importantly, his aging mother enjoyed having him at home.

Rex and Campbell had moved back in to his mother's house after his wife died. The arrangement had provided stability for his son, along with daily doses of the Bible and cod liver oil, both of which the old Mrs. Graves deemed essential for a clean and healthy life. Rex had been brought up on them too and used to pull the same faces as Campbell, either one of boredom or disgust, depending on the torment presented.

The memory brought Campbell back into focus. Rex felt sure something was amiss in spite of his son's assurances on the phone that all was well: his second year at Hilliard University in Jacksonville was going fine; he had not been troubled by his bronchitis all winter; and he was still seeing the girl Rex had met in the summer on his way to the Caribbean to look into the case of the missing actress. Campbell had never suffered a lack of female company to his father's knowledge. He was, as Helen pointed out, "a chick magnet."

It had been something in his son's tone. Rex couldn't quite put his finger on it, but he was certain he wasn't imagining things. Three months had passed since he had last seen his son, and that was a long time in a young adult's life. Still, he would be with Campbell soon, and there were things left to do in the meantime.

When his cell phone rang later that evening, he almost didn't answer it, thinking it might be Moira until he saw Helen's name on the display. "Hello there, lass," he said with a smile.

"I just wanted to wish you a safe trip. Are you all packed?"

"Aye. I'm sorry we can't be spending Easter together."

"I hope it all turns out to be a storm in a teacup with Campbell."

"What are you going to do while I'm away?" he asked.

"Spring clean my house, and then reward myself with a big Cadbury's egg!"

"Save one for me."

"I will. It'll be so nice to have a break from work." Helen was a high school counselor. "This term has been especially gruelling. Teenagers seem to be facing greater challenges each year."

"I know something's going on with Campbell, but since he won't talk about it on the phone ..."

"I understand perfectly." Helen was a reasonable and practical woman, traits he truly appreciated about her. "I imagine it's even harder for kids in America," she added, without spelling out the additional problems of random shootings and more readily available drugs. She didn't have to. Rex was thinking the same thing.

"I canna wait to see you when I get back," he told her.

"Is there anything special you want me to arrange for us to do in Derby?"

"I'd like to spend the weekend the way we did in Rosewell," he said, alluding to Christmas when they had driven to the Orchard House Bed and Breakfast in Midlothian, managing one hike to Roslin Glen. Mostly they had stayed in the four-poster bed.

Helen giggled. "Sounds good to me."

"You have the number of the motel I'll be staying at on Jacksonville Beach, and I'll have my mobile phone with me."

"Give Campbell my love."

"I will. He really enjoyed meeting you at Christmas."

"He's a terrific boy, Rex."

"I suppose we should call him a young man. He turned twenty earlier this month."

They said their goodbyes. Rex did not see the point of telling her about Moira. It could wait until he saw her. He shut off his phone and mounted the stairs to bed.

Setting the alarm for his early morning flight, he felt relieved to think that by this hour, local time tomorrow, he would be with his son in Miami.

THREE

THE PLAN WAS FOR Campbell to pick him up in Miami, where his son was spending Spring Break with his girlfriend, and then to drive up to Jacksonville together. Rex woke up in his Miami motel room the first morning fully recovered from jet lag and looking forward to catching up on his son's news on the long drive north.

As it turned out, Campbell must have been up all night saying goodbye to Consuela. He wore board shorts and had not bothered to shave. In fact, he looked like the dog's breakfast and slept most of the way up Florida's east coast in the old Chevy Trailblazer while Rex negotiated the multi-lane highway sprouting exits in all directions. He wasn't used to driving with the wheel on the wrong side. To make matters worse, Interstate 95 was undergoing road construction. Signs cut lanes off at short notice and reminded drivers that speeding fines would be doubled when workers were present. Not that any workers were present, though they had left their barriers, bulldozers, and ten-ton rollers behind.

What little scenery there was soon lost its novelty on the seemingly endless miles of straight road. Hours later, as Rex was passing the sign to Interstate 4 and Orlando, he tuned into a classic rock station that happened to be playing all his favorite songs. The traffic had cleared, and the expressway opened up before him as he listened to "Angie" by the Rolling Stones, a warm breeze ruffling his shirt through the rolled-down window. He turned up the volume and sang along to the lyrics.

"*Oh, Angie, don't you weep, all your kisses still taste sweet, I hate that sadness in your eye-eye-eyes …*"

"Why are you howling, Dad?" Groggily, Campbell reached for his bottle of mineral water.

He still looked peaky after his nap, in spite of his tan. He had inherited his chiseled features and blond hair from his mother, his height from his dad, minus a few inches. The previous night, Rex had been amused to see that he had grown sideburns. "I'm not howling," he protested.

"Caterwauling, then. Urgh, this water's warm."

"It was cold when I bought it at the petrol station. By the way, this SUV is a great big gas guzzler. Why on earth did you get something so expensive to run?"

"It's useful for stowing my boards in."

"What's first on your schedule tomorrow?" Rex asked, exasperated as always by his son's lack of financial acumen and deciding to change the subject before they got in a row.

"Stats, worst luck."

"Good lecturer?"

"Pretty cool, though not as cool as my marine science teacher."

The Americanism sounded funny in Campbell's fluted Scots accent, which was noticeably less pronounced than when he had left Edinburgh twenty months ago.

"Last night was fun," Rex said conversationally.

He had taken Campbell and Consuela to dinner. Rex secretly referred to his son's girlfriend as the Cuban Princess. A spoiled diva with an incredibly extended family that lived in South Beach, she had, as far as he could tell, little going on between her pretty, diamond-studded ears. He felt sure she was a distraction to Campbell's studies, the distance between their two colleges at opposite ends of the state adding a strain to the relationship.

They passed a green sign for St. Augustine, which Rex had in mind to visit if he had time, curious to see what the "oldest" city in the continental United States was like.

"So, what's going on in your life?" he asked, having received no response to his comment about dinner.

"The usual."

"I don't know what 'usual' is in your world."

"I told you pretty much everything last night." Campbell could be surly when he got too little sleep.

"I thought there might be something you wanted to tell me in private."

"Like what?" His son stared out the side window.

Rex checked the rearview mirror and, slowing down abruptly, pulled onto the grass shoulder lined with spindly trees. "Here—you drive." He got out of the SUV and walked around to the front passenger door. Eighteen-wheelers rumbled by at high speed.

Campbell took his father's place at the wheel. "What's the matter, Dad?" he asked as he yanked on his seat belt.

"It's been a long trip and a long week," Rex explained. "And I don't have the energy to pursue a one-sided conversation. We're approaching Jacksonville. You know where we're going better than I do."

He had decided to stay at the beach, a twenty-minute drive from the university. That way, Campbell could surf and, as he put it, "hang out" at the Siesta Inn, which had a pool and a minigolf complex next door.

Campbell eased into the inside lane. "Should we go straight to the motel?"

"Aye, I'd like to get a swim in. Then we can have something to eat and you can go to your dorm."

"Sounds good. I could pick you up after class tomorrow and we could do something. I'll be through by midday. I'm glad you came," Campbell added in a conciliatory tone.

"Me too," Rex told him. Aside from seeing Campbell, he was looking forward to swimming every day, walking the beach, and eating American fare. He could never get over how big the portions were and he liked the casual attitude toward dining in Florida.

They drove under a concrete porch into the Siesta Inn parking lot, and he went to check in at the front office. The stucco walls of the motel were painted a warm shade of ochre and decorated with Mexican pottery visible between the arched walkways. He had requested the room he had stayed in when his son first started college, located up one flight of concrete steps, with a balcony overlooking the ocean.

Unzipping his suitcase on one of a pair of queen-size beds, he extracted his Bermuda trunks. "Do you have an electric kettle I can borrow?" he asked, surveying the kitchenette. "Tea doesn't taste right when it's done in a microwave."

Campbell had opened the glass sliders to the balcony. "I think I may have one somewhere. If not, we can pick one up."

Rex joined Campbell on the balcony, which was just large enough to accommodate two plastic chairs and a table. Blending into blue sky, the Atlantic stretched in a deep shade of indigo beyond a broad swath of sand accessed by a boardwalk. White-crested waves rolled onto the shore.

While Campbell took off to the beach with his surf board, Rex walked to the motel pool to perform his laps. The fenced-in pool was heated and empty, the sun warm on his back. He missed the sensual feeling of swimming nude in the Caribbean, where he had felt as free as a fish in the sea, but this was still a huge improvement on the heavily chlorinated indoor public baths he had to make do with at home. After counting off fifty laps, he got out feeling invigorated and refreshed, and set out to join his son.

Sea oats fringed the near side of the beach, composed of powdery dunes. Farther out, the sand became more compacted, allowing for vehicles to drive up and down the shore. To the north a pier extended into the ocean. Motels, affluent homes, and older rental properties stared out to sea along the beachfront. He arrived just in time to see Campbell skim in on his board, poised like a bird for flight, and jump off into the shallows.

"Not rough enough today," his son called out, approaching with his surf board in the crook of his arm and sweeping his dripping blond hair from his eyes.

His shoulders had developed breadth from paddling out on the board, but in other respects he looked thinner than when Rex had seen him at Christmas. Campbell had complained that the food "sucked" on campus, and Rex planned to feed him up for the duration of his stay. "You're covered in goose bumps," he chided. "Go take a hot shower, then we'll get some dinner."

While he waited on the motel room balcony, he glanced through a copy of *USA Today*, which he had picked up at reception. An article caught his eye: "*Suicide Ranks After Traffic Accidents as Second Leading Cause of Death among American College Students.*" He didn't have time to finish reading the piece before Campbell wandered out of the bathroom, his narrow hips girded with a white motel bath towel.

"Hungry?"

"You bet." Campbell grinned, and Rex felt reassured.

Perhaps his son had just been going through a rough patch with Consuela, and that was why he had sounded depressed on the phone. He seemed better now and, certainly, he and his girlfriend had been lovey-dovey at dinner the previous night, feeding each other off the same plate and all but ignoring him.

The oceanfront bar and restaurant Campbell selected that evening was a far cry from the swanky joint on Miami Beach, and just what they were both in the mood for. They ordered conch fritters with mango jalapeno salsa, followed by oak-grilled New York Strip and fries, accompanied by a pitcher of beer. Campbell produced a fake I.D. upon request.

"I forgot it's illegal for you to drink," Rex admonished when the server had left. "Where on earth did you get that?"

"I'm almost twenty-one."

"You just had your birthday!"

"All college students drink. In the UK, you can consume alcohol in restaurants at sixteen."

"I'm well aware of that, but we happen to be in the States. And when in Rome..."

"C'mon, Dad. You can vote in the States at eighteen and get sent off to war."

"Well, just *one* pint. I'll drive you to the dorm."

"How will I get back here tomorrow?"

"I'll pick you up."

"That's crazy."

"You're the one who chose to come and study here. I do envy you the weather, though."

They enjoyed the rest of the meal and Rex was pleased to see Campbell polish off a wedge of pecan pie for dessert. Afterward, he drove his son to Hilliard, a small, private college on the bank of the St. Johns River.

Students were still arriving back from Spring Break, laden with bags and laundry hampers. He helped Campbell carry his belongings up the stairs to the third floor of his dorm. A single room had become available at Keynes Hall, permitting his son to pursue his second year on campus, much to Rex's relief.

The room housed an accumulation of clutter, including Campbell's other surf boards and his treasured Stratocaster guitar and amps. A poster of British soccer star David Beckham brightened one wall. Textbooks teetered in a heap on top of the scarred wooden desk, the shelves above reserved for his son's collection of shot glasses. When Campbell left for college, his grandmother had given him a homemade quilt with hexagons in contrasting plaids

—the only Scottish item in the room, other than the shot glass embossed with a thistle.

"You got a new rug," Rex noticed. "It all looks very cosy." If not very serious. In fact, it more resembled summer camp than university. "I should have taken marine science instead of law," he quipped.

"You wish." Campbell smiled in wry amusement.

"You should open the window. It's downright stuffy in here."

"The air's not working properly."

Rex took a final look around. "Right, well, I'll be going, then," he said, reluctant to leave, even though Campbell seemed relaxed and at home. "I'm sure you want to get yourself organized for tomorrow. Call me after your class."

After hugging him goodbye, he made his way along the corridor and down the stairs, avoiding collision with the rowdy male students in his path. They were a friendly lot, smiling at him and asking how he was doing in that pleasant American way. Suddenly, an echoing scream broke out on the second floor, doors banging open amid a hubbub of voices.

Rex stepped out of the stairwell and peered down the corridor where a group of students, a red-headed female among them, took turns forcing a door knob. Loud Hip-Hop pulsed from the room, adding to the commotion.

"Break down the f-ing door!" a student yelled over the din.

"What's up?" another questioned in passing, gym bag and hockey stick slung over one shoulder.

"Dix Clark hung himself," garbled a boy from the group, holding his head in both arms and pacing up and down the corridor.

"The peer mentor? Are you for real?"

"Look for yourself. There's a crack in the doorframe. Kris saw him just now. She's calling an ambulance."

The first youth ran up to the door and kicked hard to no avail. He swore again with affront.

Rex decided to intervene, though he couldn't be sure the whole thing wasn't a prank. "Did I hear someone mention a suicide?" he asked, approaching.

"My boyfriend," the girl wailed, freckles standing out from her pale skin amid a cloud of auburn hair. Cell phone in hand, she frantically pointed to the crack by the door.

Rex bent down and put an eye to it. Without a moment to lose, he grabbed the knob and, positioning all his weight, rammed his shoulder into the door. It gave way, revealing the interior scene. A boy dressed in jeans dangled from a noose attached to a central ceiling fan, his bulging eyes staring into space.

Gasps of dismay erupted behind Rex. A chair lay on its side a short distance from the boy's limp feet. Praying it was not too late, Rex rushed over and raised trembling arms to release him.

FOUR

REX CALLED FOR SOMEONE to cut the boy down from the ceiling fan, while he supported the body. A student righted the chair, jumped up on it, and untied the knot, slipping the nylon rope over the boy's purplish face.

"Is he dead?" the student asked squeamishly.

Judging by the skin color and the protruding tongue, Rex feared the worst. "The medics will be here shortly. You did just fine, lad. Help me carry him to the bed."

The body, still warm, weighed no more than one hundred and fifty pounds, in Rex's estimation. He thought he detected a weak pulse by the *V* ligature mark on his neck, but it was hard to tell with the music rapping from a boom box by the door and vibrating through the walls. As he was about to yell for someone to turn it off, he heard the words, "I'm pre-med," and made way for a young man who proceeded to massage the victim's heart and attempt to breathe air into his lungs.

Someone, mercifully, switched off the CD, and Rex could hear himself think again. For the first time since entering the dorm room, he began to take in the details. A knitted Easter bunny with "We love you, Dix" embroidered on a blue tank top sat by the bedside. Photos lined the wall, including a group of boys beneath a Phi Beta Kappa fraternity banner. He recognized the boy on the bed and another face he had seen.

The rest of the room comprised a locked single-hung window, a futon in burgundy denim, shower stall, older model computer on a desk similar to Campbell's, but arranged in a more orderly fashion, room key... As Rex was taking a mental inventory, voices suddenly rang out in the corridor, steps pounding the linoleum floor. The crowd by the door parted as a pair of paramedics rushed to the bed. Rex retreated from the room.

"Dad?" Campbell's voice roused him from his reflections. "I heard all the din beneath my room. Is he going to be all right?" He looked fearfully toward the door as the stretcher emerged.

A squawk of police radios interrupted Rex's reply. Bodies flattened against the walls to let the stretcher pass by, while a medic held breathing apparatus to the victim's face.

"Who found him?" a green-uniformed cop asked the knot of students.

"I was the first to reach him," Rex replied. "This young lady saw him through the door."

The officer questioned the girlfriend, Kris Florek, who asked if she could follow the ambulance to the hospital. A dark-haired boy with clean-cut looks came forward to explain that he had knocked on Dixon Clark's door an hour and a half earlier to round him up for soccer practice. Dixon had answered the door and seemed "spaced out." He had declined to play, claiming he didn't feel well and was going to bed.

"Was he alone in his room?" the cop asked the student, who had given his name as Justin Paul.

"Yes, sir. I stood just inside the door and there was nobody else with him."

"Where do his parents live?"

"Nantucket. He was up there for Spring Break."

At that moment, a tall man in his late fifties, dressed in slacks and a polo shirt, marched up to the door. The corridor fell silent.

"The dean of students," Campbell informed Rex under his breath.

"Thank you for responding so fast," the man told the officer in charge. "You got here before campus security."

"We were in the neighborhood."

"Who's the student?"

"Dixon Clark. His girlfriend looked in and saw him hanging from the ceiling fan."

"I'd like to go to the hospital, unless you need me for anything?"

"Go ahead, Dr. Binkley. We got it covered here."

A second cop closed the dorm room door and posted himself in front of it. Rex signaled to Campbell. It seemed ghoulish to stand around when there was nothing further they could do. They made their way down the corridor past mute faces and weeping girls seeking comfort in each other's arms.

A boy waylaid Campbell on the stairs. "Did you see anything, bro?"

Campbell shook his head and followed his dad up the steps and into his room.

"Do you know the boy who tried to hang himself?" Rex asked.

"I played soccer with him. That's about it. He's an RA."

"What's that?"

"A resident assistant. They enforce the rules and give guidance to freshmen, that sort of thing. They get to room for free."

"How old is he?"

"Don't know exactly. He's a sophomore like me. Is he going to be okay?"

"If he survives, he may have brain damage. It just depends how long his brain was deprived of oxygen."

"Jesus."

Rex sank onto the narrow bed, thinking about the article on suicide he had read at the motel before dinner.

"Do you want a dram of whisky, Dad? You look like you could use one."

"You have whisky here?"

"Glenfiddich."

"In that case, I wouldna say no." He decided to postpone inquiring how Campbell had procured whisky. Then he dimly remembered the fake identity card.

His son served the single malt to him in the shot glass embossed with a thistle.

"Thanks, lad." Rex knocked it back in one draught. The two of them sat in silence for a while. "What did that boy mean about Dixon Clark looking 'spaced out'? Is he on drugs?"

Campbell shrugged. "I don't know why Justin went and said that."

"Presumably because that's the impression he got when he saw Dixon."

"Yeah, but volunteering information…"

"He was being cooperative. What's wrong with that?"

"The cops here aren't like back home, Dad."

A knock sounded at the door. Campbell went to answer it.

"There's a candlelight vigil for Dix," a young male voice said. "On the grounds outside his room. You coming?"

"He didn't make it," another voice added. "Kris called Justin from the hospital. DOA."

Rex let his brow fall into the palm of his hand. Poor sod, he thought. What a waste of a young life. He rubbed at the corners of his eyes before glancing up at Campbell. "Go on. I'll stay here."

When the door closed, leaving him alone in the room, he stretched out on the quilt and stared up at the ceiling fan. He imagined Dixon's parents receiving the call in Nantucket. No doubt the onerous task of notifying parents fell to the university president or the dean of students. It was bad enough losing a son in a climbing or motorcycle accident, Rex reflected, but having him take his own life… The twirling fan grew hypnotic. *Mrs. Clark, I regret to inform you that Dixon was found hanging in his dorm room. He was rushed to ER but was pronounced dead on arrival. His girlfriend was by his side. My deepest sympathy for your loss…*

The room suddenly depressed him. He should take Campbell back to the Siesta tonight, he decided, looking at his watch. It was almost ten.

Half an hour later, Campbell returned from the vigil with Justin. Rex proposed that Campbell pack what he needed and go with him to Jacksonville Beach.

"I want to stay, Dad."

"Why?"

"As a show of solidarity."

"Then I'll stay. As a show of solidarity to you."

"But there's nowhere for you to sleep."

"I have a rollaway you can borrow," Justin offered.

He returned with a fold-up bed on wheels, which reminded Rex uncomfortably of the gurney that had whisked Dixon away from his dorm room.

"You take the bed," Campbell told his father. "This will be way too short for you."

The bed, once unfolded, left little moveable space in the ten-by-twelve-foot room. Campbell fetched a sheet from the closet and grabbed one of the pillows from his bed, while Justin watched from the door.

"Not exactly the Ritz Carlton," he said.

"I've slept in worse places," Rex replied. "Do you have your own room or do you share?"

A quick glance passed between the boys.

"I share," Justin said. "Well, I did before my roommate dropped out."

"Why did he do that?" Rex asked, sensing there was more to this story.

"Actually, he was expelled."

"Sounds like a lot goes on in this hall. Are expulsions common?"

"Not really. He got into some trouble. He was cleared, but the faculty made his suspension permanent anyway."

Campbell in the meantime had grabbed his guitar from its stand and sat on his desk chair tuning the strings.

"Seems a bit harsh," Rex remarked. "What was he suspended for?"

"Dealing blow."

"Excuse me?"

"Cocaine, Dad," Campbell interjected, staring at Justin as though he wanted him to shut up.

"Well, I'll say goodnight, then." Justin apparently got the hint.

"Nice lad," Rex said when he had left.

"Yeah."

"What's he studying?"

"Business."

"What does his dad do?"

"He's a stockbroker."

"What about Dixon Clark's parents?"

"I think his mother's a teacher. Not sure about his dad. I know they have a large sail boat. Dix mentioned it a few times. I don't think they're hurting for money."

"I saw a photo of a boat on his wall. Lovely lines."

"Dad," his son said regarding him with skepticism. "You know sod all about boats."

"True, but I can appreciate a beautiful shape." Constructed of polished wood, it bore the name *Providence*. God, what a horrible irony, Rex thought.

"I have a spare toothbrush," Campbell told him. "I better warn you—the bathrooms are rank."

Rex accepted the new toothbrush but didn't move from the bed. He wanted to ask Campbell if he had tried coke. The fear that he might be on drugs had been his primary motivation for getting on a plane and coming to see him. However, he decided it was a question that would have to be asked obliquely and when the moment was right. He had detected a clamming up in Campbell, and there had been enough drama tonight. "Just tell me one thing," he asked his son.

Campbell waited—warily, Rex thought.

"Do you think Dixon's death was a suicide?"

"I guess. What else could it have been?"

"I didn't see a suicide note, unless it was among the papers on his desk."

"Maybe he wrote one on his computer."

"That would seem a bit impersonal, don't you think? Anyway, his monitor was switched off. And his girlfriend looked stunned, as though his death was totally unexpected."

"So?"

"People who contemplate suicide often talk it over with those closest to them, assuming they have people who are close to them." This much he had read in the newspaper article. People who followed through on their suicidal thoughts often felt isolated and misunderstood.

"That's true," Campbell agreed, resting his chin on his guitar. "I pretty much tell Consuela everything, except the fact that I lust after my marine science teacher."

"Really? Is she that hot?"

"Her picture's on a website called StudentSpace.com. Someone blogged she worked as a porn star while she was getting her masters."

Only in America, Rex thought wryly.

"I doubt it's true, though," Campbell added.

"Then it's libel."

"Oh, you can write whatever you like. The First Amendment and freedom of speech, and all that."

"She could sue for defamation of character."

"Sue who?"

"Sue *whom*," Rex corrected.

"It's anonymous."

"Sue the website—for disseminating libelous information. That's what I abhor most about the Internet," Rex bemoaned. "There's bugger-all control over content."

"Yeah, it's way out of control."

"Did Dixon's life seem out of control?" Rex asked.

"Not really. He had to have been making decent grades and have a clean record to be selected for the RA program."

"Was he popular?"

Campbell pulled a face. "Somewhat—I guess. Not as popular as Justin, or some of the other jocks. He played soccer, but he was no star. In fact, he was a bit of a pussy."

"A pussy?"

"He never took chances."

Rex lay back on the pillow. Nothing he had heard about Dixon Clark so far made him sound like a candidate for suicide. He had a family, a girlfriend. His position as a resident assistant kept him in contact with other students. He'd just returned from Spring Break with his parents in Nantucket. Rex had never visited New England, but recently he had read Nathaniel Philbrick's *In the Heart of the Sea* about the true story that inspired *Moby Dick* and depicting the close-knit whaling community on the island in the 1800s. Dixon had a whole network of people to reach out to.

Presumably, his mother, grandmother, or sister had knitted the Easter bunny that he had placed by his bedside. A person with such strong family ties would leave a note, he was sure of it. And maybe one for his girlfriend.

Perhaps deeper forces were at work, something stronger than family and community. What was it that Campbell and Justin were not saying? There was a strange atmosphere in the dorm. He had felt it in the corridor, even before he had heard Kris Florek scream. Or was he just imagining it in the light of recent events?

No, he would trust his intuition. Something was going on and whatever it was, he didn't want his son mixed up in it. He had to get to the bottom of Dixon Clark's death for his own peace of mind.

FIVE

Rex woke up early in the stuffy dorm room. The corridor resonated with the banging of doors, putting him in mind of a cell block in a prison. Hoarse voices greeted each other as boys headed for the showers or out to breakfast. Campbell slept through the noise, sprawled over the rollaway, an arm and a foot grazing the rug. Rex got up and foraged in the small refrigerator for bottled water.

"Morning, Dad."

"Morning. I was trying not to wake you."

Yawning, Campbell pulled on some jeans. "Be right back."

He left the room and returned five minutes later looking as though he had dunked his head under the faucet.

"Can we get breakfast in the cafeteria?" Rex asked.

"Not unless you want food poisoning. The eggs are green."

"What about the ham?"

"Ha, ha."

"What do you suggest, then?"

"I can get us some coffee and bagels from Einstein Bros. Do you need a razor? I have some disposables."

"Ta."

Rex turned on the television to CNN before going to freshen up in the boys' bathroom while Campbell was out getting breakfast. His son returned with Justin. One by one, other boys gathered in the room, perching on whatever furniture was available or else sitting on the floor. Most wore sweats or board shorts and clasped cans of Red Bull energy drink. Rex sat on Campbell's bed sipping his steaming hot coffee, a wrapped bagel beside him on the plaid quilt.

"How was the rollaway?" Justin asked.

"Great," Campbell said. "Thanks for the loan."

"No problem. It's not often we have parents staying in the dorm."

"Is there a rule against it?" Rex asked.

"Not sure," answered a gangly redhead slumped against the wooden closet. "Parents usually stay in motels."

"I have a motel room, but it was more convenient to stay here last night as I don't have a rental car."

The boys stared at him with good-natured interest. Rex got the impression they regarded him as though he were a rare and exotic species at the zoo. They were probably intrigued by his accent, which was more guttural than Campbell's.

"Campbell said you were a lawyer," ventured a bespectacled boy in a wrinkled Miami Dolphins jersey.

"A barrister," Rex qualified. "Or as we call them in Scotland, an advocate. We make a distinction between advocates, who are trial

34

lawyers, and those who mainly engage in legal matters outside of court or in the lower courts, whom we term solicitors."

"Cool."

"So what are you lads studying?"

"Engineering," said the redhead, who introduced himself as Matt Simmons. "But everybody calls me Red."

In Scotland, where redheads such as Rex were common, the nickname would not have been so appropriate. "And where do you hail from, Red?"

"Boulder, Colorado."

"Must have been quite a change for you coming here."

"I guess. I like rock climbing, but I enjoy water sports too. I came mainly because of the climate."

"And what about you?" Rex asked a tow-headed boy.

"I'm from Indiana. Go Colts!" He pointed to his white thermal long-sleeve top with a blue horseshoe on the front, the significance of which Rex had totally missed, since he knew next to nothing about American football. "Business Studies, same as Justin," the boy added. "I'm Mike."

"Pleased to make your acquaintance. And what was Dixon Clark majoring in?"

"Public Relations."

"Did anyone here take classes with him?"

The students shook their heads. None of them seemed truly despondent about Dixon Clark's death, but then Rex didn't know what their usual demeanor was like. Maybe they felt it wasn't "cool" to display their emotions.

"I took Computer Science with him last year," Campbell responded with a trace of reluctance.

"Who were Dixon's close friends?"

The question met with a collection of shrugs and blank looks.

"He was in my fraternity," Justin replied. "But Phi Beta Kappa is not a real active society, and we're small. We mainly trade term papers and organize barbecues to raise funds for beer."

"Klepto, his ex-roommie, I guess," said the bookish one in the teal-on-white Dolphins jersey—or perhaps it was his glasses that made him look studious. "They were tight."

"Klepto? Is that his real name?"

"Nuh," Red replied. "His real name is Ty Clapham."

"We call him Klepto 'cause he likes to lift stuff," Mike from Indiana explained.

"He's a kleptomaniac?"

"He takes iPods, digital cameras, watches, designer sunglasses, even rims off cars, and sells them on eBay."

"Yeah, he's got really light fingers," Red elaborated. "He took my student I.D. one time. My fake one. Not that he looks anything like me. He probably sold it."

Rex had the curious sensation that he was talking to a bunch of conmen.

"One time I couldn't find my brand-new chemistry textbook," the boy with glasses chimed in. "I paid over a hundred bucks for that puppy. Turns out he listed it online."

"Did you make an official complaint?"

"We were going to once we got proof, but Dix persuaded us not to, saying Klepto had problems at home. We said okay, if he paid us back and agreed to move out of the dorm."

"That was very magnanimous of you. Where does Klepto live now?"

"In the hood, back of the college," Mike said.

"He'll be at Dix's memorial service, for sure," Red added. "He owes that dude big time."

"Yeah, Dix always had his back," Justin agreed.

Rex glanced quizzically at Campbell.

"Looked out for him," his son interpreted, picking up his books. "I have to get to class. Later, guys."

Matt Simmons, AKA Red, groaned as he staggered up from the floor. "I got an assignment due in this morning. I better go start it."

"Wanna work out?" Mike asked the chemistry student.

"Maybe later. I have to burn some CDs."

They all trooped out, leaving Rex on the bed chewing on his bagel and wondering what had happened to discussions on existentialism. These kids seemed a bit adrift.

He decided to consume the rest of his breakfast outside and made for the quad between the dorms, where two trestle tables stood among a cluster of mature oak trees. He sat in the shade of one and watched gray squirrels dart up and down the gnarled trunks, twittering among themselves.

Students, singly and in pairs, headed toward the faculty buildings across the berm dividing the six-story brick residence halls from the rest of the campus. According to the prospectus, as Rex recalled, Hilliard University had been established in the fifties and had added a theater and new labs since then, yet remained a four-year institution of fewer than three thousand students.

A jeans-clad coed split off from a trio of girls and approached him. Rex recognized Dixon's girlfriend Kris Florek from the previous evening. This morning, her profusion of auburn hair was confined in a ponytail. Her freckles, even more pronounced in bright daylight, matched the amber of her eyes.

"Hi," she said. "Did you sleep over?"

"Aye. In my son's room. How are you feeling?"

"Hard to say. I'm in shock, obviously. My academic advisor told me to take as much time as I needed, but I can't afford to miss class. Anyway, it's better to keep busy."

"That's probably true, if you can—though grief will catch up with you sooner or later." He gestured for her to sit down.

She hesitated for a second before slinging her book bag onto the wooden table and settling on the bench opposite him. "Sounds like you speak from experience."

"I lost my wife over five years ago."

"How did you get over it?"

"Time got me over it."

"I've known Dix for about five years. We attended the same schools on Nantucket, but didn't start dating until college." She caught her breath. "I don't understand it. Why he did it, I mean."

"Did he ever hint at doing something like this?"

"I've been thinking about that a lot and now I keep, like, reading things into statements he made, which I thought were innocent at the time."

"Such as?"

She tugged on her T-shirt, giving a wistful sigh. "One time I was studying in his room. Well, dozing, really, on the futon. He was working on the computer. Suddenly he got mad and started cursing. He kicked over the chair and said, 'I can't take it anymore.' I thought he'd received a really bad grade or something. He didn't like his math professor and thought he had it in for him."

"What's the professor's name?" He would ask Campbell if he knew him.

"Cormack."

Rex swallowed the last of his coffee. "What happened then?"

"Dix was pretty stressed out. He went to the Student Health Center and got a prescription for Xanax, which seemed to calm him. I was worried he might become dependent on it. Also, there is a risk of suicide with anti-depressants, although I never thought he'd actually do anything."

"Are you training in the medical field?"

"I'm at the School of Nursing here. I've barely been able to keep up, what with Dix's problems these past months. The added pressure of him being an RA didn't help. We decided to spend some time apart over Spring Break. I went to North Carolina with my roommate and he went home to Nantucket. His parents are flying in this afternoon."

"You've spoken with them?"

"Yeah. They're devastated, naturally. They wanted to know what happened. I told them I hadn't seen Dix since before he left for Spring Break and that when I got back I went to his room and saw him, you know…" Kris wrung her plump hands. Suddenly, she glanced at her watch. "Shit, I have to go."

"Take care, Kris."

Nodding hopelessly, she got off the bench and wandered off in the direction of the teaching buildings. Rex wadded up the packaging from his breakfast and threw it into a concrete trash container, and then walked on to the campus library, planning to do some research while Campbell was in class. On the way there his mind worked feverishly.

Supposing Kris was right and Dixon Clark had become suicidal from taking the Xanax? Rex felt a pressing need to acquaint himself with the symptoms of depression in young people. How could he ever hope to help Campbell if he didn't recognize the warning signs?

He had sensed undercurrents of tension from the boys in the room that morning and had realized to his consternation that he was completely out of touch with his son's generation. One student was already dead, and he couldn't help thinking that someone somewhere was responsible to some extent, though whether through ignorance, indifference, or even malice, he did not have a clue.

He could only pity the poor parents now on their way to the university, who no doubt were consumed by the same thoughts as he.

SIX

AFTER CAMPBELL'S STATISTICS CLASS, they drove along the Arlington Expressway to the Regency Square Mall, where they ate a quick lunch. Rex bought his son a few items of clothing, along with a set of microwave-proof dishware, a new feather pillow, and a clock radio. Campbell had complained of occasionally sleeping through his old alarm clock, which Rex didn't find surprising in view of the general racket in the dorms. He also insisted on buying his son a bottle of multivitamins and a stock of Florida orange juice.

It was the first time he had taken Campbell on a shopping spree, unless he counted the purchase of school uniforms and stationery at the beginning of term. Campbell's mother and, after her death, his grandmother had fulfilled that role before his son left for college.

"What made you get me all this stuff?" Campbell asked as they loaded the provisions in the back of the SUV.

"I thought it might cheer you up."

"Thanks, Dad." Campbell gave him a quick hug in the parking lot and drove them back to the campus, looking much perkier.

As they were putting the last of the stuff away in the room, Justin knocked on the door, which Campbell had jammed open with a stopper. "Dix's parents are here," he announced in a fluster. "They'd like to see you, Mr. Graves."

"Me? Do you know why?"

"I think because you were first on the scene yesterday evening and they want to thank you."

Rex felt his face suffuse with blood. His palms went moist. He didn't want to meet the grieving parents, especially to be thanked for something that any reasonable person would do; worse still, when he had not been able to save the boy. All the same, he did not see how he could refuse. "Where can I find Mr. and Mrs. Clark?"

"In Dix's room."

The three of them traipsed down the steps to the second floor, and Rex and Campbell approached #216 in the middle of the corridor. The doorframe had been repaired. When he knocked, a good-looking man with a weathered face opened the door. Rex cleared his throat and held out his hand. "I'm Rex Graves. This is my son Campbell."

"Keith Clark. My wife Katherine. Please come in."

Mrs. Clark, who sat on her son's bed clasping the Easter bunny, murmured an effortful greeting. An empty cardboard box stood on the floor by her feet.

"Please sit down," Keith Clark invited, taking the computer chair at his son's desk.

The remaining option was the rigid-looking futon in burgundy denim, which Rex and Campbell settled onto as comfortably as the poorly padded sofa allowed.

"We understand you tried to help our son."

"I wish there was more I could have done. I'm so sorry."

Mr. Clark dismissed the apology with a flutter of his hand. "We're still trying to make sense of what happened. The medical examiner said the cause of death was asphyxia by hanging. The police ruled our son's death a suicide. There's no note, but they found instructions downloaded from the Internet on how to kill yourself."

"Where were those found?"

"Here on the desk. They're from a Goth website called Necrophacts.com, which is all about death and which lists, quite graphically, the easiest ways to commit suicide."

"We feel we must have done something wrong along the way," Mrs. Clark murmured, momentarily closing her eyes while she composed herself. She shook back her sun-streaked hair, which looked as though it had not seen a brush since the previous morning. Rex's heart went out to her. "And yet he seemed quite cheerful over Spring Break, didn't he, Keith? He was out catching up with high school friends who were also home from college."

Rex remembered how Campbell had done the same thing over his Christmas vacation.

"I didn't notice anything was wrong," she continued in a monotone, twisting the knitted bunny in her hands. "We sat up late one night talking in the kitchen, just like old times when he lived at home."

"The dean of students told us that one out of every 7,500 to ten thousand college students takes his or her life each year in the States," Mr. Clark interjected. "As if it might be a comfort for us to know that our son is a statistic!"

"I suppose he was stressing the importance of not blaming yourselves," Rex ventured.

"How can we not? Did you know our son well?" Mr. Clark asked Campbell.

"Not very well, sir. We played on the same soccer team. And he was in my computer science class last year. We worked on an assignment together." Campbell seemed instinctively to understand that the Clarks would be glad of even the smallest detail regarding their son. "Everybody I knew liked him."

Mr. Clark smiled in gratitude at Campbell. "So is your dad here in Florida on a visit?"

"He came over from Scotland for the week. We're hoping to visit the Keys next weekend before he leaves."

"Do you like sailing?"

"Aye," Campbell replied. "And fishing."

"Where are you staying?"

"We don't know yet."

"We have a beach cottage in Islamorada. Dix loved it." Keith Clark smiled sadly and turned to Rex. "I read an account of the Swanmere Murders in England in some magazine. When Justin told me a Scotsman by the name of Rex Graves had broken down Dix's door, I guessed you might be the barrister who solved that case. Is detective work something you do often?"

"I was involved in another case in the Caribbean just last summer. An acquaintance asked me to look into the disappearance of the French actress Sabine Durand."

Mr. Clark nodded thoughtfully. He hesitated. "I wonder if we might ask a favor of you."

"Go ahead."

"We feel there are some loose ends in our son's death, but we're flying back home after the memorial service on Wednesday, and I don't think we'd know where to start searching for answers if we stayed. You seem like the right person to look into things for us. I know it's a big imposition on your time ..." He looked ashamed to ask, and Rex knew he had to be desperate.

"You feel there are unanswered questions," Rex restated.

"The whole thing just seems so quickly disposed of," Mrs. Clark said through fresh tears. "I can understand that the university wants to sweep this under the rug with minimum upset to the other students, but we need to feel easy in our minds that what happened to Dix could not happen to someone else's child."

"Do you suspect the university is at fault somehow?" Rex asked gently.

"Show them the letter, Katherine," her husband urged.

She reached into her bag and drew out a couple of sheets of paper. "If Hilliard is in any way responsible for my son's suicide, I want to know!"

Her husband took the documents from her and handed them to Rex.

"Did you show these to the dean of students?" Rex asked after glancing at them.

"He said the college was looking into it."

45

"It's a bit late for that," Mrs. Clark remarked.

Rex reread the ditty that someone had posted on StudentSpace. com under a thread entitled The Snitch.

> *There once was a man from Nantucket*
> *Who kept all his stash in a bucket,*
> *A student named Ray*
> *Got framed one day*
> *And the man from Nantucket said fuck-it.*

Dixon was clearly the man from Nantucket, but who was Ray? He asked Campbell. His son shrugged in reply. And what did the "stash" refer to? Was Dixon involved in drugs?

"Has the ME performed a toxicology test yet?" Rex asked Keith Clark.

"The report showed traces of Xanax, which we knew about."

Next, Rex perused the copy of a letter their son had sent to Hilliard University a month before, demanding that the Student-Space website be shut down, or at least that all malicious references to him be deleted. "Campbell, didn't you mention something about a website called StudentSpace.com?"

His son stiffened beside him on the futon. "It's a site where students post gossip about their faculty and peers. It's a place to vent and let off steam, but it's become really ugly. There are accusations of students being gay or promiscuous and professors in AA, and stuff like that."

"Dix was being harassed," Keith Clark said.

"You'd think the university would want to shut it down," Rex commented. "It's hardly conducive to harmonious relations between students, and between students and staff."

"The dean said it was almost impossible to track down the main culprits," Mrs. Clark explained wearily. "He said a social website similar to StudentSpace.com started at Harvard. He went on about Hilliard being a liberal college and freedom of expression and blah-blah-blah. I told him that if the website was responsible for my son's death I would sue Hilliard for negligent failure to intervene and prevent it. Dr. Binkley said the college never received a copy of that letter." Katherine's taut expression suggested she didn't believe it for a moment.

"You think the dean might be lying," Rex said with a sympathetic nod.

"I think it's a big cover-up."

"We're not saying there might not have been contributing factors," Mr. Clark clarified. "Just that this website may have pushed Dix over the edge, if he was already in a delicate frame of mind. I mean, that's a pretty vicious poem someone wrote accusing our son of abusing drugs—if I'm reading it right."

His wife let out a shuddering breath. "We knew about the Xanax. Dix said it was for anxiety. The pressure of his studies was getting to him and he was falling behind in math. He took Xanax before his SATs and then quit afterward with no ill effects, so we weren't too concerned. When I found that poem and the copy of the letter he wrote to the college in his bedroom at home after he left, I knew there was more to it. I've been wondering if he meant to show them to us and then changed his mind."

"I guess what we're asking of you is that you find out what you can and maybe let us know our best course of action," Clark told Rex. "If, of course, you agree to help us."

"As you know, I am not able to act in any legal capacity since I'm not licensed to practice law in this country," Rex cautioned.

"We realize that. But you'd know what questions to ask, and Campbell has inside knowledge of what goes on here on campus."

Rex glanced over at Campbell, and his son nodded, indicating his willingness to help.

"I'm here until the end of the week. I'll give it my best shot," Rex promised.

"As to compensation ..."

"Not necessary. As a parent myself, I feel I have a stake in this too."

"Well, at least let us give you the loan of our cottage in the Keys. There's a small fishing boat you can use, and a couple of kayaks ..."

"Och, that seems like too much responsibility—"

"Dad," Campbell objected. "I have my boater's license."

"It's an eighteen-footer, center console with a ninety-horsepower motor. Campbell won't have any problem with it. We have a beauty of a sail boat back home. This other one is just for dinking around."

"This is very generous of you," Rex said.

"Not at all. There's a realty office across the road—Islamorada Vacation Homes. Ask for Donna. She keeps a spare key for when our friends stay at the cottage. We'll call her and let her know to expect you. The office is open every day until six." Mr. Clark reached into his jacket pocket and pulled out his wallet. "Here's my business card. Please call if you find out anything about what we discussed." The card was inscribed with the words, *Clark & Associates. Architects*. "The memorial service will be held at St.

Peter's Episcopal Church, Wednesday at four. We'll be returning home afterward."

"With our son's body," Mrs. Clark added, crumpling onto Dixon's bed and hugging his pillow to her face. "This still smells of Dix," she sobbed into it.

Rex worried what impact this might be having on Campbell. He was distracted by a knock at the door. Mr. Clark, who had risen to go to his wife, opened it. A young girl with an arresting face and long, caramel-colored hair flew over to Mrs. Clark and knelt down by the bed to console her.

"Our daughter Melodie," Mr. Clark said. "She's a freshman at BU."

"We won't impose on your grief any longer, Mr. Clark," Rex said, getting to his feet. He turned toward his son who was staring at Melodie with a look of awe and compassion. "Campbell."

"Oh, aye." Breaking out of his trance, Campbell rose from the futon and shook hands with Mr. Clark. "Thanks for the loan of the cottage and the boat."

Mr. Clark nodded. "Glad to see them go to good use."

Melodie gazed inquiringly at her dad from where she knelt on the floor.

"This is Campbell, and his father, Rex Graves. They'll be spending the weekend in Islamorada."

Melodie smiled weakly at Campbell. "Hope you have a nice time. It's beautiful down there."

Campbell looked at his feet. For the first time, to Rex's knowledge, he seemed at a loss for words in front of a girl. And then he did something surprising. Crossing the room, he crouched down in front of Mrs. Clark and took her in his arms. Rex turned away as tears pricked his eyes.

"My dear boy," he heard the mother say. "Thank you so much."

Campbell stood up and, with a quick goodbye to Melodie and Mr. Clark, left the room.

"He lost his mother when he was fifteen," Rex murmured by way of explanation before following his son out the door. Catching up with him, he put an arm around his son's shoulder. "You okay, lad?"

"I hope I didn't act like an idiot in there. It just seemed like the natural thing to do."

"Then it was the right thing to do. I think Mrs. Clark appreciated it. She's probably been thinking how hard it's going to be not to feel her son's arms around her again. Come on. I could do with some coffee."

Rex felt he could really do with something stronger, but coffee would have to suffice. He needed all his wits about him if he hoped to make headway in Dixon Clark's death by the end of the week.

SEVEN

"THANK GOD FOR THIS place," Campbell said to his father as they stepped out of the campus Einstein Bros. "I could live on these cinnamon raisin bagels. In fact, I practically do."

They sat on the circular wall of a fountain and sipped their coffee while students sauntered past in animated groups, carrying textbooks and binders under their arms.

"Did you notice her eyes?" Campbell asked.

"Whose?"

"Melodie's. They're violet."

"I noticed she had a very expressive face. I thought her parents were an attractive couple. They seem like very nice people."

"Poor old Dix must have lost out in the gene pool. Not that he was bad-looking, but Melodie … wow." Campbell bit thoughtfully into his bagel.

Rex wondered if this meant the swan song for Consuela and the Cuban mob. "What is BU?"

"Boston University."

"That's rather far, isn't it?"

Campbell thumbed a glob of strawberry cream cheese off the side of his mouth. "It's in Massachusetts."

"Like I said. Far."

"It's not as though I was going to ask her out."

Rex slid him a look. "I just wondered because you have that dreamy look in your eyes."

"I admit I was smitten, but she's in mourning. Even if I wanted to—and Consuela wasn't in the picture—it would be totally inappropriate."

Water trickled soothingly from the fountain behind them as they sat in companionable silence for a while, watching industrious squirrels forage among the blooms of a tall red maple.

"This place is overrun with squirrels," Rex noted.

"Raccoons too."

"It's grand that the Clarks are letting us have the cottage. It simplifies our weekend plans no end. I just hope this investigation isn't going to interfere with your studies."

"It won't. What do you want me to do to help?"

"I'm not sure yet. I'll probably just be sounding you out about things. We'll see how it goes. First, I'd like to speak to the faculty member who would know Dixon best."

"Try Astra Knowles, the school registrar. You'll find her in that building back there. She knows everybody. Can you ask her about the school bereavement policy while you're at it?"

"What do you mean by a bereavement policy?"

"It's when they make academic concessions for the students who knew the deceased…" Campbell seemed embarrassed, as well he should be, Rex thought. "The boys were discussing it."

"The lad's dead, and you lot are trying to find ways of taking advantage?"

"I know…but most colleges have some sort of policy. We're just curious."

Growling in disapproval, Rex stood up. "Say we meet back at your room at five?"

"Sounds good. I have band rehearsal this evening so we won't be able to have dinner. At least, not until late."

"That's okay—I wouldn't mind going back to the motel and having an early night."

Much would depend on whether he got hold of Ms. Knowles, and what he could find out about Dixon. His parents had entrusted him with an important task and he was determined not to let them down.

Fortunately, Astra Knowles was available and able to see him right away. A statuesque woman of middle years, she wore a white blouse billowing over a long batik skirt, and silver hoop earrings.

"I understand you want to see me about Dixon Clark," she said with a puzzled look on her smooth brown face.

"I'm here *in loco parentis*. Mr. and Mrs. Clark asked me to look into possible motives for their son's suicide."

"You're a friend of theirs?"

"I was referred," Rex said evasively. "I'm a lawyer back home in Scotland. But I do investigative work on an *ad hoc* basis."

"You like Latin phrases, huh?" Ms. Knowles smiled in amusement.

"I have the Clarks' number if you wish to verify," Rex said, a trifle discomfited that she might find him pompous.

She gestured for him to sit down. "That won't be necessary. I'll try and be as helpful as I can without stepping outside my job description. Love your accent, by the way. It's cute."

"Er-hm, thank you."

He settled into a metal-legged chair across from her desk. Tall file cabinets of monotonous gray surrounded the desk on three sides, many of them punctuated by incongruously decorative fridge magnets depicting all manner of things from fruit to fish, some of them appended with notes.

"These file cabinets are my babies," the registrar said, following his gaze. "I been at Hilliard twenty-three years. Ain' nothing I don' know about scholastic policy. You ask me for a student's academic record, I can put my hands on it in under a minute. Now, you probably looking around thinking, 'Bureaucracy! I'm gonna be stonewalled by rules and regulations 'til I can't see straight!' But see here?" Astra Knowles pointed to a plaque on the wall. "'Efficiency NOT Bureaucracy!' That's the code I live by."

Rex felt not so much stonewalled as marshmallowed. He was getting nowhere, but in the pleasantest possible way. "Did you have much interaction with Dixon?" he asked.

"Some. This is a small college. I know most students, if only by sight. Most of the boys I know by name. They're the ones I see most."

"Do you know a Ray?"

"Got a last name?"

Rex shook his head.

"Yeah, boys are the worst offenders," Ms. Knowles remarked, shaking her tight black curls. "They come in here all the time begging to drop out of classes if the going gets tough. Give them an easy way out and they'll take it. They find a class where they don't have to write papers, they jump into it like lemmings. When a website called StudentSpace.com went live, listing the softest graders and the easiest courses to pass, there was an epidemic of transfer requests. But I do have a special place in my heart for boys, having two of my own—grown men now. Lazy as the day is long, they were, but they doing all right for themselves now."

"Was Dixon a good student?" He would start with the basics and see how far he could get.

"Average. He definitely benefited from the small classes we have here at Hilliard. But he was a D bordering on F in math."

"Did he request a transfer?"

"Sure did, but I couldn't get him out of his class as David Green's was full."

"So he stayed with Mr. Cormack." Rex leaned forward in his chair. "How can I reach his math professor?"

"I'll see if I can get him for you." Referring to a typed pull-out list of names on her desk phone, she punched in a number. "Al? Astra here. There's a gentleman in my office named Rex Graves who would like a word with you about Dixon Clark...Sure thing, hon. Thanks." She replaced the receiver. "He's on his way."

"Thank you. I also wanted to ask you about another student, Kris Florek, a nursing major."

"I have the School of Nursing files right here. Has this something to do with Dixon Clark?"

"She was his girlfriend."

Ms. Knowles hesitated at an alphabetized file cabinet. "I ain't authorized to give out information on just any student. Dixon

Clark's case is different, since you are acting for his parents and the poor kid is dead."

"I understand." Rex decided not to risk pushing his luck. "What is the policy regarding students who were close to the deceased?"

"You mean a bereavement consideration?"

"Aye—credits for non-attendance and such."

"We have guidelines, but each case is judged on its own merit."

"Have you had many cases of suicide?"

"Only one other in my time here. It happened off campus. A student jumped from a building. Usually, concessions are only made for a roommate or a girlfriend or boyfriend. But we have grief counselors available for all affected students."

"What sort of concessions would those be?"

"A passing grade for the semester if needed. We don't want to add to a student's duress and have to deal with another tragedy."

At that moment, a young man in pressed jeans and a blue striped shirt entered the office.

"Al, this is Mr. Graves. I have an errand to run down the hall. Take my chair, hon."

Mr. Cormack sat opposite Rex and smiled pleasantly. "How can I be of help?"

"I'm here at the request of Dixon Clark's parents who, understandably, are trying to comprehend the reason or reasons behind their son's suicide."

"And you think it might be because he was failing in math?" Cormack asked with a raised eyebrow.

"I want to determine what sort of pressure he might have been under in general. Studies, girlfriend, peers, finances, anything at all."

"Well, I don't think blame can be put on me. I try to be fair. If I see a kid struggling but coming to class and turning in his work, I bend over backward to give him or her a passing grade, or at least a bit of latitude with regard to retaking a test."

"Did Dixon try?"

"Yeah, he did."

"And yet he was a borderline F."

Cormack's face reddened. "Okay, but he got the grades he deserved."

"Meaning?"

"Where are you going with this?"

"I'm simply trying to get at the truth."

"The truth is Dixon Clark got another student in trouble for something he didn't do, and he wasn't man enough to own up to it. I don't reward bad ethics."

"Would you care to elaborate?"

Cormack fidgeted with a cube container of paper clips on Astra Knowles' desk. "Another student of mine got busted for dealing drugs and was suspended. There was no proof beyond Clark's camera phone video. Turned out it could not have been R.J. on it. But he was expelled anyway, mainly on Clark's say-so. And because he was unable to explain why he couldn't get his hands on the hoodie he owned, supposedly the one on the video."

"But wasn't it Dixon's job as a resident assistant to report drug activity?"

"It's part of his job, sure, but R.J. was acquitted by a jury, and I felt the university should've gone with the verdict. Instead they sided with Clark. R.J. Wylie was an A student in math, although he was actually a chemistry major. I strongly opposed the university's decision and almost got fired."

Cormack was practically hyperventilating now. He looked at his watch and excused himself. "I'm meeting my girlfriend. Good luck."

After he left, Rex sat in his chair pondering the professor's reaction while he waited for Astra Knowles to return. The Nantucket ditty began to make more sense as he mentally recited it.

> *There once was a man from Nantucket*
> *Who kept all his stash in a bucket,*
> *A student named Ray*
> *Got framed one day*
> *And the man from Nantucket said fuck-it.*

Cormack had said Dixon got R.J. in trouble for something he didn't do, and wasn't man enough to come forward.

If one went with the facts, as one must, there could be no doubt that Dixon had taken his own life, since the door and window were locked and instructions on how to commit suicide were found on his desk. There was no sign of a struggle in the room or on the body, and no one in the corridor had seen or heard anything suspicious, except that the RA was playing his music louder than usual.

So what had driven Dixon to end his life? Remorse for getting another student in trouble?

After getting nothing further out of Astra Knowles, Rex crossed the campus and returned to Keynes Hall to meet Campbell. He did not have a key to the building, but a student who was entering the main entrance let him in without hesitation when he explained he was a parent. Despite his size, Rex did not present a threatening figure. Helen had described him as cuddly. This reminded him of his resolution to exercise each day that week, regardless of how busy he was. He would do his laps as soon as he got back to the motel.

In the meantime, he ran energetically up the first flight of stairs, walked the next two, and made his way slightly out of breath to his son's room, where he opened the door and found Campbell and Red waiting for him. The gangly redhead was beating a pair of drumsticks against Campbell's desk.

"You must be the drummer in the band," Rex said.

Red nodded and sent one of the sticks cart-wheeling into the air, catching it with a nonchalant twirl of his wrist.

"What did Ms. Knowles say?" Campbell asked.

"Not much, except that a roommate or a really close friend of a deceased student would receive a passing grade for the semester if they needed it." Rex joined Campbell on the bed.

"Lucky for Kris then," Red remarked. "She was flunking out of Nursing School."

"She's got to be taking it hard," Campbell said.

"Dunno about that. They had a big bust-up before Spring Break and she wasn't talking to him."

Young love, Rex thought as the boys debated the question of Kris' feelings for Dixon. He considered mentioning what the math professor had told him, but didn't want to advertise the fact that he was talking to faculty members about Dixon's suicide. "Anyway," he said, getting up. "I'll leave you lads to it. Good luck with band practice."

"You should come and listen one evening, Dad."

"I'd like to. Have you got a name for the group?"

"Dirty Laundry."

"'Cause we play down in the basement where the washers and dryers are," Red explained.

Rex grinned. "Must make for some interesting background accompaniment."

"It's hell," the boy replied. "It really throws you off."

"Campbell, can I take the Glenfiddich with me? I thought I'd have a wee drink out on the motel balcony. I'll replace it if necessary."

"Help yourself."

"Ta. Bye now."

He descended to the car park and, getting into Campbell's SUV, drove to Jacksonville Beach, managing to miss the worst of rush-hour traffic. The glowing orange sign welcoming him to the Siesta Inn beckoned with the promise of a quiet night in a clean and comfortable bed.

By six-thirty, he had been for a swim and was ready to leave the motel room for a solitary dinner pondering his notes on the case when an urgent knock sounded at the door.

"Moira!" he exclaimed upon opening it, scarcely believing his eyes. The woman he had left on Arthur's Seat stood on the walkway with a small suitcase, dressed in a cotton print frock and a knitted bolero cardigan, in spite of the warm evening air. The clothes looked like they came from a thrift shop, but somehow suited her gamine-like figure. Waiflike was the word that had often come to mind in the days he had thought about Moira.

"Are ye not going to let me in?" she demanded as he stood there in shock.

EIGHT

Without conscious thought, Rex stepped aside so Moira could pass. She deposited the suitcase on the carpet and sat on the far bed looking out at the view of the ocean through the balcony rail. Rex watched speechless as she slipped off her clunky-heeled shoes and lay prostrate on the zigzag patterned bedspread.

"I can hardly believe I made it all this way and found you so easily."

Neither could Rex. "So how did you?" he asked, perching on the other bed and wondering what he was to do.

"The young man who devils for you told me where you were staying. I told him it was an emergency. And so it was."

It had never occurred to Rex to tell Angus to screen his calls. He had left him the number of the Siesta Inn in case a colleague needed to contact him. Never in his wildest dreams had he thought Moira would follow him across the Atlantic. "Why did you come?" he demanded.

"I told you before. I have to talk to you. I'm trying to put my life back together."

"Well, I've moved on. I thought I had made that perfectly clear in Edinburgh." He gave a heartfelt sigh. "I'm afraid you've wasted a trip."

"I dinna think so. This is an ideal opportunity to clear things up. I prepared a speech, but I've forgotten it." She smiled ruefully at him, displaying sharp little teeth.

"It's not as ideal an opportunity as that," he protested. "It so happens a student at Campbell's university hanged himself, and the parents have asked me to look into it."

"Why you?"

"I was first on the scene."

"You always were dependable and steady, Rex. I always appreciated that about you."

"Not that much, evidently, since you ran off with the first man who looked at you twice!" Rex was surprised at the resentment that still smoldered within him. He thought he had long since put his feelings toward Moira behind him.

"That's not true!" She jumped up and paced the room. "There was a car bombing at the Sunni-Shiite neighbourhood market where I was buying provisions for the refugee center. I canna describe the deafening explosion, all the glass shattering everywhere."

"Moira…"

"People were screaming. Blood was spattered all over the dirt streets and across the buildings. Two pickup trucks arrived to carry away body parts." Moira paused, clutching at her cardigan.

"'Tis a terrible experience to live through," Rex commiserated.

"Aye." She lay back down on the bed, seemingly exhausted, and took a deep breath. "Neil was with a reporter shooting a documentary. They ran to the scene and helped excavate the victims. A shop front collapsed and buried me under the plaster. Neil lifted the door off me. I escaped with minor cuts and bruises, but what I saw that morning won't heal. I keep reliving it in my mind. There were babies, Rex, catapulted out of their mothers' arms. Oh, God!" Her legs curled into a fetal position and she began to cry pitifully.

Rex poured a glass of whisky from the bottle he had appropriated from Campbell's room. Moira was teetotal, but he felt she could benefit from it for medicinal purposes as she was clearly distressed. "Have you sought psychiatric help?" he asked, handing her the glass.

To his astonishment, she sat up and downed the whisky in one gulp. "I thought I'd be fine once I got home, but everything's changed. I want us to get back together, Rex. I need stability."

Moira had no family to speak of, and had not seen her abusive alcoholic father in years. Her main support group was the Charitable Ladies of Morningside, where she had met his mother and with whom she used to play bridge. She was *persona non grata* with his mother now. No wonder Moira was clinging to him as to a life raft. She had no one else.

"I'm sorry I caught you at a bad moment, with that student hanging himself," she murmured. "I know how he must have felt. I've had despairing thoughts too."

Rex sat beside her and took her hand. "I'm sorry I did not listen before, but this is right awkward. I'm seeing someone else."

The room phone rang.

63

"I have to take this. It might be important." He went over to the bedside table and picked up with, "Hello—Rex Graves."

"Rex! I'm glad I caught you." It was Helen. The timing couldn't have been worse. "I didn't want to try you on your mobile in case you were out doing something with Campbell."

"How are you, lass?"

"Missing you. Are you having a good time? How is Campbell?"

Rex glanced at Moira who was watching from the bed with tight-lipped suspicion and he turned his back. "There's been a crisis at the college with one of the students. Campbell's coming through it okay, I think. A boy in his hall was found hanging in his room."

"Oh, how awful! It's a very susceptible age. Young people take things so hard. They have the pressure of exams, relationships, being away from home, and the constant worry of whether they'll measure up in the real world."

Rex decided this was not the time to get into a discussion about the case even though Helen, as a counseling professional, could have offered a helpful perspective. Moira's presence in the room inhibited and distracted him. He felt frustrated at her for coming and at Helen for phoning at that precise moment.

"I could fly over," she offered. "You know, to provide moral support. I've been looking at cheap flights online. I could get a package deal to Orlando."

"Och, it's not necessary. At least not for Campbell. They have a crisis centre on campus and grief counselors available for the students. But it's not as though he was that close to the boy."

He heard a squeak of bed springs and turned around with the phone pressed to his ear. Moira crossed to the dressing table and helped herself to another drink, which she dispatched with as much speed as the first. She refilled her glass. Rex knew he should terminate the call with Helen, but felt guilty at fobbing her off.

"But what about you, Rex?" Helen asked. "I could be there for you."

"I appreciate that, lass, but I'm busy looking into a few things to do with the boy's death. I'm convinced there's more to it than meets the eye. I feel like I'm on a personal crusade. The boy was Campbell's age."

"It brings it home, doesn't it? When someone in your immediate circle dies."

"Don't mind me!" Moira exclaimed in a loud voice, planting her small frame by the phone between the beds.

"Who's that?" Helen asked. "I'm sorry. I didn't know you had company."

"It's Moira. She visited unexpectedly." He avoided eye contact with his guest.

The silence at the other end of the line was painful to hear.

"Moira Wilcox?" Helen asked finally.

"Aye. She came to see me in Edinburgh on Friday. And she turned up just now at my motel."

"You make me sound like a bad penny!" Moira exclaimed.

"You didn't tell me that on Friday evening when I phoned," Helen reproached him.

"It didna seem important." As soon as the words slipped out of his mouth, he regretted the stupidity of his remark. "I'm going to make sure she gets back safely on the next flight home."

"I'm not a UPS package!" Moira remonstrated. "And I'll not be spoken about as though I weren't here!"

Clearly the whisky was getting to her. She plunked down her glass on the bedside table and grabbed the phone before Rex knew what was happening.

"This is Moira," she told Helen. "And I have no intention of leaving. I knew him before you did, and for longer. And he told me he doesn't love you. Goodbye!" She slammed down the phone as Rex looked on in horror.

The damage Moira had just inflicted on his relationship with Helen was immeasurable, maybe even irreparable.

"I don't think I can ever forgive you for what you just did," he said in a cold flat voice, resisting the urge to grab her by the throat.

"What does it matter?" Moira shrieked. "It's all over anyway." She hurled her empty glass across the room at the mirror above the dressing table, which splintered into a thousand pieces and showered down on the carpet like rain.

To Rex it seemed symbolic somehow.

NINE

Moira needed help; that much was evident. Rex desperately wanted to call Helen back and explain the precarious situation, but he could not risk doing so while Moira was still in the room.

"I'm sorry," she said, suddenly deflated.

"I know. You're tired from the journey and not used to alcohol. Why don't I see if I can get you a room so you can sleep it off?"

"Why can't I stay here? There are two beds."

"One is for Campbell when he stays over."

"I dinna want to be alone in this strange place," she said, her speech slurred. "I shouldna've come. I feel disorientated, like I was back in Iraq."

"Well, lie down on the bed for now while I go to reception and sort out a few things."

"Do you mind if I take a bath first?"

"No, go ahead. Will you be okay?"

"Can you bring me something to eat?"

She looked like a lost child, standing in the room by her suitcase. His heart ached in pity.

"There's a Chinese take-out down the road."

Moira's face brightened. "I adore Chinese."

"I remember. I'll get the green tea if they have it."

"Rex ... thank you." Her brown eyes begged him for forgiveness.

What a mess, Rex thought as he left the room. He didn't look forward to explaining to the motel staff about the mirror, but they would have to send someone upstairs to clean up the glass before Moira stood on a jagged piece and hurt herself. He jogged down the concrete steps and crossed the softly sunlit parking lot. The bell on the reception door tinkled as he opened it. He took a preparatory breath. The middle-aged woman behind the counter glanced up at him with a courteous smile.

"I have a situation," he began. "First, I need to report a broken mirror."

Her face registered restrained surprise. "Did it just break?"

"No. A woman I used to know followed me from Scotland. She got a wee bit carried away."

"Oh, she came in earlier. Short brunette? Sorry I gave out your room number. She was very insistent."

"I'm afraid she's not well. She just returned from Iraq."

"Combat duty?"

"Charity work, but she was caught in a bombing. She's behaving irrationally. I need to arrange a flight for her back to Edinburgh in the morning, if at all possible. Can you take care of that?"

"Sure. Coach or first class?"

"Whatever is available. Preferably non-stop." He didn't want Moira changing her mind and flying back.

Then he left a message for his mother, asking her to send someone from the Charitable Ladies of Morningside to meet Moira off the plane; he would call again later with the flight times. Moira could spend tonight in the spare bed, he supposed.

Now for the food. He drove to the Red Dragon, where he ordered fried rice, chicken-cashew, and spicy beef and broccoli. "Oh, and a few packets of jasmine tea," he asked the cashier.

When he got back to the SUV, he thought about calling Helen from his cell phone, but he didn't want to leave Moira alone too long and let the food get cold.

By the time he returned to the room, the glass had been swept up and the mirror replaced. He called up reception to applaud the motel's efficiency. Moira was singing in the bathroom to the accompaniment of water splashing in the tub. He found a couple of plates in the kitchenette and took them, along with the plastic knives and forks, to the balcony table. He then went back inside to boil water for the tea, wondering if he dared call Helen while Moira was in the bathroom. He doubted Helen would be asleep even at the late hour in England, but ultimately decided to wait until he had more time. All he needed to do, he told himself, was to keep Moira calm and get her on the next flight out in the morning.

She came out of the bathroom, her hair straight and wet, her thin shoulders glistening above the white towel wrapped around her torso. "I hope you don't mind, but I used up all the Pro Terra products."

"The motel will replenish the stock. Are you ready to eat?"

"I'll just slip into my bathrobe. Are we eating on the balcony? How lovely."

Rex brought the cartons of Chinese food to the table. The restaurant had thrown in two spring rolls and a couple of fortune cookies. Unfortunately, he no longer had much of an appetite.

Moira joined him in her pink robe and lifted the tea bag out of her mug. "Pity we don't have a candle. It's nice out here, isn't it?"

The ocean gleamed dark and remote beyond a scattering of silhouetted palm trees, yet the scene failed to stir any romantic feeling in Rex.

"You couldna do this in Baghdad. There's a curfew at night and the temperature can drop dramatically."

"It must be difficult living out there," Rex said, helping himself to the chicken-cashew.

"Aye, you never feel safe, even in the Green Zone. What surprised me most was the Iraqis going about their daily business with an air of resignation, in spite of all the disruption to their lives."

"I don't suppose they have much choice."

Moira ate fast and abundantly. It had always amazed him that such a small person could put away so much food. He suspected a lot of it went on nervous energy.

"What does your fortune cookie say?" she asked at the end of the meal.

He peered at his slip of paper. "Mine's fruity: 'You will gain admiration from your pears.' Is that really Confucius?"

Moira laughed. "Mine says, 'Riches are measured in friends.'" She read it in a Chinese voice, and Rex laughed in turn. "It's true though," she said, gazing intently at him.

"These must be the writers who failed the greeting card class," he remarked with forced levity.

"Let's take a walk along the beach."

"Aren't you tired?" He wanted Moira to go to bed. She seemed uncharacteristically exuberant, much like an overexcited child at a theme park, and it made him uncomfortable.

"I'm getting my second wind. A moonlit walk along the beach would do me a world of good. At least do that much for me after I came all this way," she pleaded.

The room phone rang at that moment, and Rex picked it up in trepidation. It was the front desk calling with information about flights. When he got off the phone, he told Moira he had booked her on a Continental flight leaving from Jacksonville International Airport at 8:30 A.M.

"You should have let me see if I could change the flight on my airline."

"This has just the one connection—in Newark."

"I'm a free woman. You didna need to go making arrangements to get rid of me so fast, as though I didna have a say in the matter!"

"You don't," Rex said firmly. "You can come back to Jacksonville for a sightseeing visit when I'm not here."

Moira sat back in her chair, a fixed look in her eyes. "Well, I suppose there is no point in staying if you're going to be like that."

"I'm going to be occupied at the university over this business with the Clark boy, and I want to spend time with Campbell."

"Very well, but I'd still like to go on that walk."

Moira was nothing if not willful. Rex could see no way out of it and, in any case, was starting to feel guilty now that he was assured of her leaving the next day.

"That's a good idea," he capitulated, clearing the empty cartons from the table. "I need to walk off this dinner."

"Save the spring rolls in case we get peckish later." Moira walked to the door.

"Aren't you going to change?"

"I'm comfortable in my robe, and it's dark. Nobody is going to notice what I'm wearing. I don't even need sandals, do I? There's a path all the way down to the sand."

Rex grabbed the room key and followed her outside. Perhaps if he walked fast he could tire her out sooner. She must be jetlagged. Then, when she went to bed he could call Helen.

His cell phone rang as they reached the beach. Moira stopped with an impatient sigh.

"Dad, I thought if you're not busy you could drive over and pick me up, and we could watch a Pay-Per-View back at the Siesta and knock back a few beers."

"Sounds like a glorious idea," Rex told his son with regret. "But I have company. Moira flew in and surprised me."

"The woman you were dating? The one who went to Iraq?"

"Aye."

"Does Helen know?"

"Unfortunately."

"Jesus, Dad. You're in for it."

"I'll take a rain cheque on the beer and movie."

"When's she leaving?"

"Tomorrow."

"That's too weird."

"I'll call you in the morning. Night, Son."

"You should take off your shoes," Moira suggested as he pocketed his phone. "The sand feels wonderful."

"I'm fine with them on," Rex replied shortly, resentful that he could not spend the evening with Campbell. "Well, let's get on with this walk."

"Dinna be like that. I'll be gone tomorrow. Look at that sliver of moon. It's so balmy out, with just enough of a breeze." She shook back her hair, which had dried to its natural waviness.

Rex strode off down the beach. Moira made no attempt to keep up with him. She strolled along dreamily, from time to time dipping her bare feet in the rushing waves that left a lace of foam on the shore. When he could only make out the pale shade of her robe in the darkness, he stopped and waited for her to catch up, wondering whether they would eventually end up in Daytona if they walked far enough south. At night, the sand gave an impression of infinity, rolling out toward an ever-receding horizon as he continued to walk almost hypnotically.

"You win," Moira called after him.

"I didna mean for it to be a race. I'm just preoccupied."

"I can see that. Let's get back. Can you remember where the motel is? It's awfully dark."

Two miles down the beach, Rex recognized the awning at the entrance to the boardwalk. They regained the room and Rex went to brush his teeth.

"I have Tylenol PM if you need help getting to sleep," he said when he came out of the bathroom. He set the alarm for 5:45 A.M.

"Where is it?" Moira asked.

"In the medicine cabinet."

They were the soft gel kind, and Rex hoped it would take effect quickly. He took advantage of her absence in the bathroom to leave a brief message for his mother.

"I took two," Moira told him, slipping into the other bed in her robe.

Rex stripped to his boxers and turned off the light. He wished Moira goodnight and lay listening to her breathing, at the same time calculating what time it would be in England. Once he was sure Moira was asleep, he would slip out of the room and call Helen, even if it was just to leave a message. As he was composing the words in his head, he drifted into sleep, awaking only when, hours later, an insistent *beep-beep-beep* interrupted a dream where he was waving Moira off at a misty gray train station.

Reaching out groggily, he turned off the alarm and looked over to see if she was awake. He discerned her dark form under the covers though he could hear no breathing. He rolled out of bed, wishing he could have slept longer.

"Moira, time to rise and shine. Do you want to use the bathroom first? I'll make coffee."

When no response came, he went over to the bed and shook her arm. He encountered something wet. He frantically called her name while he fumbled for the light switch. Blinking in the sudden glare, he saw pools of blood either side of her body where she had cut her wrists. Clammy fear engulfed him as he dialed 9-1-1 from the room phone.

After stating his emergency, he ran to the bathroom for hand towels and bound her wrists as best he could. He tapped her cheeks. Her eyes flickered open and closed heavily.

"Moira! Stay with me. The ambulance is on its way." In a fold of the sheet he spotted his razor. "For God's sake, why did you do it, Moira?" he cried.

He grabbed her by the shoulders, and she moaned. He just had time to pull on some clothes before he heard a siren break the silence. He drew back the drapes. A sickly dawn was beginning to rise over the ocean.

TEN

Rex paced up and down the waiting room. Finally, he sat down on a plastic bucket chair and called Helen.

"Hello?" she answered.

"Helen, it's me. Listen, I wanted to call you back last night."

"Did Moira spend the night with you?"

"In my motel room, yes."

"I see."

"No, you don't! I'm at the hospital. She tried to commit suicide. The medics think she'll pull through. I'm waiting for the doctor."

"What happened?"

"She slit her wrists."

"My God. Is she in love with you?"

"I don't think it's that. She survived a bombing in Iraq. I think she's become unhinged. She was behaving strangely last night."

"What did she mean when she said you didn't love me?"

"I told you—she's sick. She became violent and broke a mirror. I had booked her on a flight home, and now this."

"It sounds to me like she doesn't want to give you up."

"Helen, I do love you. I cannot tell you what a relief it is to be talking to you."

"I don't know what to say. I was stunned to find out you were seeing her again."

"I wasn't seeing her! She just turned up. She called my chambers and found out where I was staying."

"This is a big mess, Rex."

"I know." Rex crumpled in his chair. Fortunately he had the waiting room to himself.

"It's a lot of information to process. I mean, is she always going to be a part of our lives—assuming she survives? I'm not sure I could handle that."

"She won't be."

"What about the guilt? She'll wreck things one way or the other."

It was unlike Helen to be so negative about a situation, but Rex understood her point of view. She realized all the ramifications of what was happening better than he did, since she dealt with individuals under severe stress on a daily basis.

"I know what you're saying, Helen, but I don't feel she has any rights on us. And I don't feel guilt—not really."

"Does she have family?"

"No. No one she can depend on." He heard Helen sigh at the end of the phone and hated what he was putting her through.

"What about the man she met in Iraq?"

"He went back to his wife."

"No doubt that and the trauma of living in a war-torn country triggered this breakdown. Sorry to sound so clinical. I want to feel sorry for her, but I can't."

"I know. I no longer have feelings for her beyond basic human compassion."

At that moment, the doors swung open and an Asian woman in a white coat gazed expectantly at him. "Mr. Graves?"

"The doctor's here," he told Helen. "I'll call you later."

"I'm Dr. Nancy Yee. Moira is going to be fine, but I want to keep her under observation for a few days."

"What about her wrists? Will there be scars?"

"Minimal. They're not deep. I don't believe this was a serious attempt. Women are three to four times more likely to attempt suicide than men, while completion rates in men are three to four times higher. I think in Moira's case it was more of a cry for help."

Rex found himself wishing Moira could have made her cry for help on the National Health Service back home, which wouldn't have cost him a penny.

"I would recommend that she talk to a psychiatrist," Dr. Yee continued. "Does she have health insurance?"

"We're visiting from the UK. I don't know if she has travel insurance or if it would even cover this. I don't suppose you offer tourist discounts?" he joked.

Dr. Yee smiled. "I wish."

"Can I see her?"

"She's sleeping now. Why don't you come back this afternoon?"

Rex returned to the motel. It was too late to cancel Moira's flight. The plane would be in the air by now. He called his mother and explained that Moira would not be arriving in Edinburgh for another few days, and why. His mother unhelpfully reminded him of a movie she had seen called *Fatal Attraction*.

"Glenn Close gets her claws into Michael Douglas and willna let go," she warned him. "Of course, it was his fault for being unfaithful to that nice wife of his. What was her name? The one with the dark, arched eyebrows. You know what Glenn Close did with the bairn's wee bunny? Boiled it alive!"

"It's only a film."

"Reginald, now ye be careful. A scorned woman is a dangerous thing. And slitting her wrists like that … It's a sin against God: Genesis 1, 2, and 9, and Exodus 20, verse 13."

"Aye, Mother. Dinna fret yerself." Mental strain thickened his Scots accent. "Moira's in hospital for now, being well cared for. I'll be in touch with the new flight times."

Rex got out of the SUV and crossed the motel parking lot. A man staffed reception. "We had to charge a new mattress to your room," he informed Rex. "The blood seeped through the bedding. Is the lady going to be all right?"

"Yes, but she has to stay at Arlington General for a few days."

Rex thought he saw an expression of relief pass over the desk clerk's face. He had to admit he was relieved too. The hospital could watch over Moira while he got on with the investigation of Dixon Clark's death.

Interesting what Dr. Yee had said about men being more likely than women to follow through on a suicide … What could have pushed the young man to kill himself when Moira, who had witnessed a massacre and been disappointed in love, had not been able to go all the way?

Rex consulted his notes and decided to visit the Student Health Center and see if he could talk to the person who had prescribed the Xanax to Dixon. Campbell had given him a map of the campus, and Rex found when he got there that the medical facility was housed in a converted block of old science labs located a quarter of a mile from the administrative buildings. The interior was set up like a regular practice, with a young pony-tailed woman in pale blue scrubs seated behind a window.

"Can you tell me the name of the doctor who was seeing Dixon Clark?" he asked her.

"The dead boy?"

"Aye. His family has asked me to look into his suicide, and I thought his doctor might have some insight."

"Why aren't his parents contacting us themselves?"

"Because they're busy dealing with formalities such as funeral arrangements," Rex said tersely. "I have their number for you to call ..."

Disregarding Mr. Clark's business card that he held out to her, she picked up a phone and pressed a button. "Becky, are you free?" She briefly explained the situation to the person at the other end. "Becky Ward," she told Rex, "is our nurse practitioner. She saw Dixon Clark."

The receptionist propelled herself in her swivel chair to a file cabinet and pulled out a folder. "She's just finishing up with a patient. I have to get a signed release from Dixon's parents faxed to us."

Rex claimed a chair by a giant potted plant and waited. A boy whom he recognized as Mike, the fair-haired business studies major from Indiana, exited a door studying a leaflet on STDs, followed shortly afterward by an older woman in a white coat. She had cropped gray hair and wore glasses suspended from a chain around her neck.

"Please come in," she told Rex, taking Dixon Clark's folder from the receptionist.

Her office walls displayed colorful charts and anatomical diagrams. A glass door offered a view of a small concrete courtyard surrounded by oak trees.

"Do you mind if we step outside?" she asked Rex. "I was about to take my lunch break."

"Please, go ahead. I'm sorry to be interrupting. It's good of you to see me at such short notice."

Carrying a Styrofoam cup and a brown paper bag, the nurse led the way out the glass door and settled on a bench against the brick wall of the building. Two squirrels leaped up beside her and raised their paws to their chins, chattering excitedly and twitching their tails.

"Little beggars," she said fondly, feeding each a piece of her salad sandwich, while Rex sat at the far end of the bench and watched in amusement. "Meet Tricky and Lola, my lunch companions."

"They're a lot more prepossessing than some of my lunch companions back in chambers."

"You're from Scotland?"

"Aye, Edinburgh."

"My grandmother was from Dunfermline."

"Oh, aye? That's not far from us."

Becky Ward gently shooed the squirrels off the bench. "Off you go now and let me eat in peace. So, Dixon Clark," she said, swiping her fingers against each other to dislodge the crumbs. She opened the folder. "This is a very sad business. He came to me for something to calm his anxiety. I prescribed an anti-depressant, Xanax, which he'd taken before."

"Did he discuss his problems with you?"

"Some." She reviewed her notes. "He said he was having problems in his social life and was having trouble sleeping. He also presented with itchy blisters on his privates, which I diagnosed as Herpes Simplex II. I wrote out a script for an antiviral. I'm telling you this because the symptoms and stress of having an STD were adding to his anxiety. I told him it was just a variation on the cold sores some folk get on their mouths and not life-threatening, but it's not easy for people to accept they have an incurable sexually transmitted disease."

"Poor kid. Is it highly contagious?" Rex wondered if Campbell knew about the virus.

"Extremely, even if you use protection. It's passed via skin to skin contact. Some people are asymptomatic and don't know they have it, and then pass it along."

"Did his girlfriend Kris Florek ever come in for treatment?"

Becky Ward picked up her coffee. "I'd need a signed release form from her before I could discuss her case with a third party. Perhaps you could just ask her, if it's part of your investigation?"

"I'd feel a bit awkward doing that. I'd be embarrassed to discuss STDs with my own son."

"I know, but parents should. Kids do listen a lot of the time."

"Sounds like Dixon had a lot on his plate."

"Yes, otherwise I might have hesitated to prescribe Xanax. Some kids use it as a recreational drug. They refer to it as Bars, Handlebars, Zanbars. It's a Benzodiazepine class of drug that lowers inhibitions. In teenagers and young adults, where the frontal lobe of the brain is not fully developed, it can lead to them acting out on suicidal and violent impulses."

"So, naturally, you monitor its use."

"Any responsible medical practitioner would. Unfortunately, online pharmacies are proliferating like rabbits, and anybody can get hold of legal prescription drugs and abuse them."

"What is the answer?" Becky Ward was a no-frills nurse of the old order, and he was interested in what she had to say.

"There needs to be better education and awareness out there. The pharmaceutical industry should stop promoting their products like they were candy. Some of these drugs are as harmful and addictive as cigarettes, but it's going to be another long, uphill battle to get the message across."

"So there is a risk of suicide if Xanax is prescribed for anxiety?"

"There is a risk, but if a kid came for help as in this case and we didn't offer it, and the kid went ahead and committed suicide, we could be sued just the same. Xanax is a helpful tranquillizer in most cases."

"One final question: Does it surprise you that Dixon Clark committed suicide?"

Cocking her head to one side, the nurse practitioner thought for a moment. "On the whole, yes. He seemed like a well-grounded young man."

ELEVEN

By the time Rex arrived back at the hospital, Moira was sitting up in bed watching TV, her wrists neatly bandaged, her dark curly hair contrasting with the starched white pillows. He placed the pot of yellow mums he had bought for her on the bedside table. Not a very inspiring choice, and she looked disappointed. He had called 1-800-FLOWERS to order the wreath for Dixon's memorial service and had tried to reach Helen, but had encountered her answering machine. He felt tired and dispirited.

"Busy day?" Moira asked.

"I was at the university talking to people." Rex didn't want to bring up the word "suicide" in her presence.

"Did anyone come up with anything helpful?"

"Maybe."

"You don't want to talk about it because you think it will upset me, but I'm curious. I don't know the lad but, from what you told me at dinner last night, he seemed to have a lot going for him. Some kids just don't know how lucky they are."

Rex hoped Dixon's suicide had not given Moira the idea of cutting her wrists. He had not realized the depth of her despair until it was too late. "You have a lot going for you too," he told her, sitting on one of the visitors' chairs.

"Like what?"

"You're still young. You do commendable work helping others."

"I'm alone. If my life was completely fulfilling on its own terms, I wouldn't need to plug the void with charity work. My life's a house of cards. It took only a couple of puffs to blow it down, and now there's nothing left."

"If we had been really strong, would you have gone to Iraq? I always felt your work was more important to you."

"I was wrong."

Rex didn't know what else to say. Moira was at the bottom of a personal abyss. "Have you spoken to a professional yet?" he asked.

"Aye, I had my 'evaluation.'"

"And?"

"They didna tell me. The staff call me by my first name as though I were a helpless wee bairn."

"Americans use first names more than we do. The doctor seems very nice."

"Nice, nice, nice! I think I'm going to scream. I hate all this bloody cocooning!"

Rex wondered if he should ring for a nurse.

"Don't worry. I'm perfectly calm," she said through clenched teeth. "They sedated me. The mums are nice. Extremely antiseptic. Thank you."

Rex sat miserably in his chair, grateful when minutes later a female orderly wheeled in a tray of food and put it within Moira's reach.

"I'm not hungry."

"You lost some blood, honey. You don' eat, you won' get discharged."

"Please eat," Rex begged.

Moira lay back on the pillows. "I dinna have the strength."

"I'll feed you." He drew up his chair and lifted one of the dish covers on the tray.

The orderly winked at him and went on her way. When he looked up, bright tears were sliding down Moira's pale cheeks.

"Don't leave me, Rex," she implored. "I couldna bear it."

He saw Dr. Yee pass the door, her white coat flapping behind her. "I'll be right back," he told Moira as he dashed out the room.

"Dr. Yee!"

She turned around and smiled briskly, tucking a stray strand of jet-black hair behind her ear.

"Doctor, I need to ask you about Moira's mental state. Can you tell me how she's doing in that regard?"

"I consulted with the hospital psychiatrist. Moira is suffering from Post Traumatic Stress Disorder. We're seeing it in an alarming number of servicemen and women returning from the war. It's a major adjustment to return to normalcy after what they've been through, and a lot of times they wind up committing crimes and acts of domestic abuse, also suicide. Moira's case is not dissimilar. She is reacting to the trauma she experienced in Iraq."

"Here's my dilemma," Rex said heavily. "I need to get her back home and I canna go with her. Is she fit to travel alone on a plane?"

It floored him to think that they should be discussing a usually intelligent and resourceful woman in this way.

Dr. Yee pursed her lips. "Perhaps if you put Moira in the charge of a flight attendant. I could prescribe something to keep her calm on the plane."

"Aye, but she has a stop-over, and I don't want her to miss her connection."

"They have airline staff to watch over children. That would be my suggestion."

"Thank you, Doctor. When can she leave the hospital?"

"Thursday morning, if she continues to do well."

Dr. Yee flew off down the corridor, leaving Rex to wonder if he dared risk booking Moira on another flight. He knew the responsible thing would be to escort her home, but he had come to Florida to be with his son and he was looking forward to their trip to the Keys, just the two of them. On top of all that, he had promised to review Dixon Clark's suicide and he did not have time to spend babysitting Moira.

At that moment, a nurse approached him. "The patient in room 403 is asking for you."

With a weary sigh, Rex turned back and entered the room.

"Where did you rush off to so fast?" Moira demanded.

"I went to have a wee word with the doctor. Are you going to try some of this Chicken Alfredo? It looks right tasty."

"Eat it yourself then. I'll have the jelly. They call it Jell-O over here. Isn't that funny? Why don't they just call it jelly?"

"Because jelly is their word for jam."

"Well, why don't they call jam 'jam'? Then they could call Jell-O 'jelly'!" Moira threw her spoon down on the tray.

"No need to get agitated over the word for a pudding."

"I am not agitated about that. It's you being all patient and reasonable! Treating me like a bairn, like the rest o' them!"

Rex wanted to tell her she was indeed behaving like a child, but he did not want to provoke another tantrum. If she had a breakdown, he would never be able to put her on a plane on Thursday.

"What did the doctor say, then?"

"She said you were recovering from PTSD, which is—"

"I know what PTSD is," Moira snapped. "What am I supposed to do about it? I can't just make it go away. And I refuse to become dependent on happy pills."

"When you get back to Scotland, you can see a therapist."

"I suppose you're already scheming how to get me on a plane back home at the earliest opportunity!" She glared at him, her face flushed with anger.

Rex swiveled the table out of the way before she could throw something at him. "What do you expect me to do?" he asked in desperation.

"Stay with me," she pleaded.

Fear numbed his limbs. He would have run if he could and never looked back. For the first time in his life, he understood the real meaning of pressure. He picked up the pocket-size Bible by the bedside and opened it to the wafer-thin page marked with a gold ribbon. He started to read aloud to her, but the words could have been in a foreign language, so unfocused were his thoughts. He held her hand until she grew drowsy. Her eyes finally closed.

The nurse assured him she would now sleep comfortably throughout the night. Slipping from the room, he regained the corridor and made his way along the squeaky linoleum to the elevators. He could not wait to get out of the hospital, with its pale green walls and smell of disinfectant. It was a relief to reach the warm air outside.

He went straight to the college and found Campbell in his room with Justin listening to a Hip-Hop CD with a catchy synthesized refrain.

"Fancy a bite to eat?" he asked them. They were dressed in button down shirts as though in anticipation of an invitation to dinner.

"Great. Where?" asked Campbell.

"Somewhere close."

"How about Smokeys?" Justin said. "It's a rib joint."

"Grand." Rex was glad of the opportunity to eat with the boys. He had several matters to clear up in regard to the Clark case and hoped they might be able to help.

Smokeys, a short drive away, was a ranch-style building located near a strip mall.

"No alcohol," Rex warned as they trooped inside.

A hostess showed them to a booth and supplied them with menus.

"How's Moira doing?" Campbell inquired.

"I suppose the answer to that is, 'As well as can be expected.'"

"So this chick just followed you out to the States?" Justin asked in apparent admiration. Campbell must have filled him in on the details. "And she slit her wrists to get your attention?"

"She's wacko," Campbell said. "Did the motel charge you for the mirror?"

"Aye, and for a new mattress."

"Gross."

"She's been diagnosed with Post Traumatic Stress Disorder," Rex offered in her defense.

His son slowly shook his head. "It's all that charity work and religion. I think she's repressed."

The server brought the beer and two Cokes. Rex ordered baby back ribs with baked sweet potato and apple sauce.

"We're still going to the Keys, aren't we?" Campbell asked when the waiter left.

"I hope so. Moira's being discharged the day after tomorrow. I'm praying she'll be well enough to travel home."

"Have you found anything out yet about Dix's suicide?" Justin asked.

"I spoke to Al Cormack. He looks surprising young to be a mathematics professor. Anyway, Dixon doesn't appear to have been one of his favourite students. Unlike a certain R.J. Wylie, whom he seems to think was the bee's knees."

Campbell and Justin stared at the table.

"All right, lads. There's something you're not telling me. I sensed it last night when we were discussing roommates."

"What did Mr. Cormack say?" Campbell asked.

"That Dixon snitched on R.J., who proved to be innocent of the drug-dealing charge. So why are you two not talking?"

"R.J. was my roommate last year," Justin admitted. "We all knew he was using. He was arrested and suspended in October of last year and acquitted at the beginning of this month."

Rex whistled in surprise. "That was a speedy trial."

"His dad hired a top lawyer who moved for a fast trial so there would be minimum disruption to R.J.'s studies. R.J. was a good student."

"So I hear."

"But he was never reinstated. The college felt where there's smoke, there's fire. They decided to make an example of him. There's a zero tolerance drug policy on campus. Using is grounds for immediate expulsion. There was a lot of controversy," Justin went on to explain as the server set a plate of barbecue ribs in front of him. "Students were divided into two camps: those that supported Dix and those that supported R.J. It was debated back and forth on StudentSpace.com. You wouldn't believe the mud-slinging on both sides." He took up his fork. "Boy, am I going to demolish this."

"And which side are you on? Or were you on?—since one of the candidates is no longer in the running."

Justin sighed thoughtfully. "R.J. was my roommate again this year. He wasn't a pusher, but, yeah, I knew he was doing drugs. It was beginning to affect him."

"And you?" Rex asked his son, who had kept quiet and was now attacking his steak and fries as though he had not eaten in a week.

"I never knew R.J. that well. Dix was okay. But if he gave the cops the video of the drug transaction knowing it wasn't R.J. all along, then that's just plain unethical."

"That's the word Cormack used. And Dixon took the video on his cell phone?"

"Yeah, he gave it to campus security, who passed it on to the police."

"Was he the first person to report R.J.?"

Campbell shrugged. "It was his job as RA."

"And yet Cormack is adamant that Dixon was in the wrong," Rex pondered aloud.

Justin mopped sauce off his mouth with a paper napkin. "He's sore about his girlfriend showing up nude on SS.com."

"What has that to do with Dixon?"

"He thinks Dix posted it in retaliation for the bad grades he was getting in math," Campbell said. "After R.J. was acquitted, bloggers began accusing Dix of starting the rumor about Ms. Johnson being a porn star. It all sort of snowballed."

"Is this Ms. Johnson your marine science professor?" Rex asked his son, remembering what Campbell had told him about her.

"Yeah. She and Cormack are dating. Dix posted a video of them holding hands and leaving together in Cormack's car. Then the nude photo of Ms. Johnson appeared. Dix denied posting it. But after his videos incriminating R.J. and exposing Cormack's relationship with Ms. Johnson, it was kinda hard to believe him."

So Cormack had a double grudge against Dixon, Rex reflected. And his best student had reason to have the biggest grudge of all, having Dixon to blame for his arrest and expulsion. Clearly StudentSpace.com had stirred up a hornets' nest for all three. It was crucial he find out who was at the bottom of the malicious gossip and if StudentSpace.com was a contributing factor in Dixon's death, as the Clarks believed, in which case they might have a chance at suing the school. Rex wanted to make sure they had the appropriate information in order to pursue any recourse that might be available to them.

"Who runs StudentSpace.com?" he asked the boys.

"Nobody really knows," Justin said.

Rex wondered if anybody really cared.

TWELVE

Early the following morning, Rex was back at the college, eager to pursue his inquiries. Motives for wishing Dixon dead were beginning to emerge. If he had committed suicide, the question was why? If someone had murdered him, the question was not only why, but who? And how? The dorm room had been as good as hermetically sealed. No one had seen anyone go in or out.

As Rex was climbing the stairwell at Keynes Hall, he ran into the Clarks, who were on their way down from the second floor.

"I was going to check in with you today," Rex told them. "I've spoken to certain members of the faculty and with the nurse practitioner at the Student Health Center, and also to several students."

"What can you tell us?" Mrs. Clark asked. She wore a little make-up today and looked more composed, although her eyes were red-rimmed.

"I still have a long way to go. The information is disjointed at present. I'd prefer to give a more conclusive report at the end of the week, if I may."

Many facets of the case troubled Rex, and he hoped to eliminate a couple of leads so that he might never have to bring them to the Clarks' attention.

"We appreciate what you're doing," Keith Clark said.

"I'm glad to be of help. It's proving to be a real eye-opener and giving me insight into my own boy."

"We enjoyed meeting Campbell."

"How are things with you?" Rex asked sympathetically.

Katherine Clark gave a weary shrug. "We're officially excluded from Dix's room 'pending further investigation.' We already took all his stuff out except for his computer. But there's a silk tie we gave him for his high school graduation that we couldn't find. Maybe he lent it to somebody. We really just wanted to say one final goodbye. If Dix had died in a car accident, we could have put a cross by the side of the road and left flowers."

"What is this 'further investigation' about?"

"The school said it wanted to keep Dix's PC for the time being and would ship it to us at a later date. Can they do that? We were going to donate it anyway as it's old and too bulky to take back with us. Keith and I also felt Dix wouldn't have wanted us to go on his computer and pry."

"Well, I don't think we could anyway as we don't have his password," Mr. Clark pointed out.

"I suppose other students will occupy his room as though nothing ever happened," Katherine said wistfully. "Well, perhaps it's for the best."

"The university probably has a computer expert who can hack in," Rex said in response to Keith's comment. "Although it seems like a lot of effort to go to. I wonder what that's all about. I think if it's not a police investigation you could probably take the PC, since it's your son's personal property."

"I must have given Dr. Binkley a scare when I mentioned suing the school over not shutting down the website," Katherine explained. "They are probably looking for evidence to pin Dix's suicide on someone else's shoulders. Oh, let them have the damn computer. I'm too tired to argue. They changed the lock on the door, so I guess they mean business."

"Maybe now they will shut down the site," Keith added. He seemed as spent as his wife. "Our daughter looked up StudentSpace.com on her laptop. I can't believe the stuff that's posted there, and the language! I expected better from a school that charges the fees it does."

"I'll look into it," Rex said, giving Keith Clark's shoulder a friendly squeeze.

"The memorial service is at four o' clock today," Katherine reminded him.

"See you there." Rex continued up the stairs, puzzled by the university's reaction, which to his mind seemed like an admission of guilt, not to mention an unnecessary additional upset to Keith and Katherine Clark.

Campbell answered the door in his boxers, his unruly blond hair sticking up in tufts. He let his father in the room and collapsed back into bed.

"No class this morning?" Rex asked.

"Not until eleven. I was studying for a bio test until two this morning. I had 270 questions to answer and memorize."

Campbell had always been a last-minute crammer, in spite of Rex's best efforts to promote the benefits of advance planning and preparation. Somehow, Campbell always managed to pass, but it infuriated Rex that the Bs his son typically received could be As if only he tried a bit harder. The biology textbook lay open on the desk, the other tomes neatly stacked to one side.

"Where would I get a plan of the residence hall?" Rex asked.

"What for? I can tell you where everything is."

"Do you realize your room is directly above Dixon Clark's?"

"So?"

"Did you lend anyone your key while you were away?"

"Justin."

"Were those books on your desk in a messy pile when you left for Miami, or were they neat and tidy like now?"

"Dad, give over. I want to sleep for another half hour."

"This may be important. You said you wanted to help."

Sighing, Campbell flopped over in bed to face him. "I noticed my books were dislodged when I got back Sunday night. I figured I had bumped into my desk when I was packing to leave for Miami. Try the housing office at Student Affairs for the plan," he added. "And bring me a bagel. Please."

Rex knew he would get nothing further out of his son for the time being. In any case, it was still early and he reasoned that the office that dealt with accommodation would not be busy with students yet, if they were all late risers like Campbell. This might be a good time to get what he needed. He left the residence hall and crossed the campus to the main administrative building, looking forward to a cup of coffee and a bagel after he had run his errand.

Almost an hour later, he was making his way back to the dorms with Campbell's bagel and a set of mechanical plans for the second and third floors of Keynes Hall. Over breakfast at the coffee shop, he had studied the trunk and duct layout. Wall and ceiling spaces were drawn in with detailed dimensions, the supply and return air grills in the ceiling of each room clearly marked.

He had also discovered from the housing office that Campbell's predecessor had been none other than R.J. Wylie, who had occupied #316 his entire freshman year. It had been a productive morning so far. The next step required Campbell's cooperation.

"Thank you!" his son enthused on receiving his breakfast. He sat in bed in his boxers to eat it. "Are those HVAC plans?"

"Aye. I struck gold. All while you were sleeping."

"Congratulations, Dad. How did you get them?"

"I used my Scottish charm."

Campbell choked on his coffee. "Yeah, right. I suppose the real question is *why* did you get them?"

Rex plunked himself down on the computer chair.

"Think, lad. Wake up."

"Someone escaped in the ducts? Ha! That's what happens in corny movies."

"Not exactly. My theory is someone used the ducts to get *into* the room below."

"Why did no one think of that before?"

"Everyone assumed Dixon killed himself. Suicide is not so very uncommon in colleges. His door and window were locked, and he had the key. The doors aren't self-locking. Suicide instructions were found on his desk. His friends knew he had reason to be depressed over being labeled a snitch on the student website."

Campbell absently scratched his crotch. "You're saying he didn't kill himself after all?"

"I'm saying it's a possibility that needs to be explored. Dixon had a few enemies."

Campbell pondered this for a few seconds. "True, and the cops were probably only too happy to write his death off as a suicide and leave the college to deal with it. They have their fair share of homicides in Jax. Seems like every day there's a knifing or shooting in the rougher neighbourhoods. So, how come you thought of the ducts?"

"I didn't, at least not consciously, until I started thinking about how there might be good reason for someone to have murdered Dixon. When I found out that R.J. Wylie had this room in his first year, I felt I might be onto something."

"I never knew that. But I never hung out with him."

"Anyway, it was just too much of a coincidence to ignore when you consider he had a compelling motive for wanting revenge. Dixon Clark was, after all, responsible for getting him expelled."

"Yeah, but R.J. couldn't have murdered Dix. He's a really laid-back sort of guy."

"You said you didn't know him that well."

"I saw him around. He was one of the popular party kids."

"Who knew you were going to be absent from your room on Sunday night?"

Campbell reached for the container of coffee on the floor. "Justin. He's the soccer captain. I told him I couldn't make practice because I was picking you up in Miami."

"He may have told his ex-roommate, Ray Junior."

"Is that what R.J. stands for? He never called himself Ray. I don't even know where he is now. What makes you think Justin is still in touch with him?"

"They were roommates this year. It's quite possible they still talk. We need to find out if we can get into Dix's room from here as the plan shows. But I want to see this infamous website first."

"Help yourself."

"Can you get me on?"

"Okay, but then I need to get to class." Campbell heaved himself off the bed and tapped around on the keyboard. "Here you go. Welcome to SS.com."

Rex scrolled down to the ditty, posted anonymously under The Snitch thread. Explicitly sexual versions followed, some of them quite comical. Campbell then clicked onto a photo gallery of Hilliard faculty and enlarged a naked image of a pretty blonde posing sideways with one leg raised on a stool and projecting an impossibly large bust.

"This is your marine science professor?"

"Uh-huh."

No wonder Cormack was upset. What man in his right mind would want his girlfriend's body viewed by thousands of horny students? "Can contributors to the site be tracked?" Rex asked.

"I suppose up to a point, but anyone could post from another student's computer—say, when the person was out of the room. Or if you knew someone else's 9-digit student I.D. and password, you could steal their identity."

Campbell then ran a short video of an individual in a gray hooded jacket exchanging a small packet of something for cash with a man in jeans and a sweater. They were too far away to show any distinct details and the video had been shot on an overcast day in the shadow of a tall building.

"Is this the phone video that got R.J. Wylie arrested?"

Campbell nodded. "R.J. was allegedly the one in the hoodie, but he said he didn't own one exactly like it and, in any case, he was signed in at a lab on the other side of campus at the time."

"Who's the other person?"

"A police informant. It was a set-up."

While Campbell got dressed, Rex read a blog on Dixon Clark's suicide. Commiserations had poured in, but many of the comments prior to his death were highly inflammatory. R.J. Wylie fared better in the discussions and appeared to have a large female following.

"R.J. We miss you!" Signed Sxylips.

"Bring back R.J.! I love u 4ever." Alabamagurl

"Dixon Clark is a snitch. R.J. rules." Lissa

Some of the coeds had included photos of themselves or else cute cartoon representations.

"Do you think you could get into Dixon's computer?" Rex asked Campbell, who was in the process of tugging a comb through his hair.

"I think so, unless he changed his password. He gave me access to his PC when we were working on a computer science assignment. I ended up doing all the work and saved his ass."

"I need you to see if you can find anything that might incriminate the university. And look for anything that gives clues as to why Dixon ended up dead." Rex explained that the PC had been as good as confiscated by the university, but he hoped it was still in Dixon's room.

"And you want me to rappel into his dorm through the air vent? Isn't that trespassing?"

"We wouldn't have to if the university was being reasonable. They closed off his room. If you stand on your desk, you can crawl into the ventilation shaft and hopefully locate the duct to his ceiling."

"I don't have time now. I have to get to my test."

"I know, but we have to do it before the computer is hauled away. My guess is the dean will wait until after the memorial service and the Clarks have left for Nantucket."

"The service is at four."

"I'll meet you back here before two. That'll give me time to see Moira at the hospital." Rex felt duty bound to see her. She did not have any visitors and must be bored to death. "Not a word to anyone about the, er, ..."

"Breaking and entering? What if I get caught? I could be expelled."

"Then you can continue your studies at Glasgow University, where you should have gone in the first place."

Campbell picked up his backpack by the desk. "I knew it," he joked. "This is just one big conspiracy to get me back home, right?"

"Kidnapping would have been easier." Rex gave his son an affectionate "nuggie," hooking his arm around his neck. "Good luck with your test."

He followed Campbell out of the room and headed for the hospital, hoping against hope that Moira would be fit enough to travel the next morning.

THIRTEEN

As Rex approached the hospital room, a somber-clothed couple hurried out the door. Moira's face, by contrast, looked illuminated. A copy of *The Watchtower* lay by her bedside.

"I've brought you a hamburger," Rex told her cheerfully. "I thought some red meat would be just the thing."

"That's grand—I'm starving."

"You have more colour in your cheeks today. You must be on the mend." He took a seat. "I see you had company."

"Jehovah's Witnesses. Did you know they're against blood transfusions?"

"Is that a fact?"

"I tried to reason with them."

No wonder the couple had looked so harried. Moira could talk the hind leg off a donkey when she got into her stride.

"I can tell the case is coming along," she said. "You have that look you get when you're about to pull one over on the defense."

"There might be a breakthrough. I'll know more after lunch."

"So you canna stay long?" She set aside her wrapped hamburger as resolutely as though she were going on hunger strike.

"I only have two more days until I take Campbell to the Keys."

"Can't I come along?"

"I need this time with my son, Moira. Besides, the Charitable Ladies are expecting you. I was not supposed to tell you this, but they're planning a welcome home party in your honour." It had been his mother's idea. "They want to hear all about your work in Iraq, and Heather Sutherland wants you to stay with her for a few days."

"That's nice of her. I'd hate to have to go back to my lonely flat."

"No need for that. She has plenty of space at her house. She'll meet you off the plane."

"Am I leaving tomorrow?"

"If I can arrange it."

"All right, then, I'll go, but you have to promise to visit me when you get back to Edinburgh."

If it meant getting Moira on the plane, he was willing to grant her wish. "I promise," he said. "I'll want to see how you're doing. Now, are you going to eat that hamburger?"

He filled her water glass as she unwrapped her burger and chatted with her while she ate it. His mind was on other matters and it was only with the greatest difficulty that he covered his impatience to leave. When he finally did, he got on the phone and made arrangements for her flight. Then he called his mother with the new arrival time, so she could relay it to Mrs. Sutherland.

"Can ye be sure she'll be on this plane?" his mother asked.

"God willing. Unless she suffers a relapse."

"How is she?"

103

"She seems stronger, both physically and mentally. But she really should see a specialist when she gets home."

"Heather has one lined up who was recommended by her brother. How is the weather in Florida?"

Rex did not tell his mother he had barely had a chance to enjoy it. Not wishing to worry her, he had omitted to mention the case of the boy found hanging in his dorm, though no doubt she would find out about it soon enough once Moira was back in Edinburgh. "It's sunny every day," he told her, and assured her he would be in contact again at the end of the week.

Aware he was running late and that there was little enough time before the memorial service to accomplish everything that needed to be done, he sped back to the university. Letting himself into Campbell's room with his son's spare key, he saw that his son had gone ahead with the plan. The desk had been moved and the grill was propped inside the opening to the air vent.

Rex stepped from the chair onto the desk. Placing his head in the opening, he called out softly, the cold dry air carrying his voice up the chute. A string wound around a nail trailed into the darkness. He could not follow it. If he pulled himself into the shaft he might get stuck. Campbell was lithe and athletic. Rex wasn't.

He thought about posting himself by Dixon's door, in case someone came to take the computer while Campbell was in the room, but decided that would only draw attention to them. He sat swiveling on Campbell's chair, straining his ear for sounds from the ceiling. He gave the Enter key on the laptop a little tap, and the surf photo screensaver gave way to an essay question that Campbell was working on. Rex took a peek.

"Many biologists claim the earth is not a living organism. However, I agree with James Lovelock that the earth is the largest living thing in our solar system. Earth is living, just like you and me.

"All aspects of the earth have biotic traits. The oxygen in the atmosphere, which we breathe and exhale as carbon dioxide, benefits the trees, which in turn benefits us. The planet has water, which gives and supports life. Earth has many similar characteristics to living organisms. It even scars and bears wounds from the damage we have caused ..."

His cell phone rang, interrupting his reading, and he fumbled in his haste to open it.

"Dad, where are you?" Campbell asked in a hushed voice.

Rex wanted to tell his son he was sitting at his desk, moved by the passion and poetry in his essay response. However, this wasn't the moment. "I'm in your room. What did you find out?"

"I reviewed the list of the last three hundred sites Dix visited. No history of access to any suicide site. R.J. could've downloaded the how-to instructions from his own computer and brought them with him. Dix accessed StudentSpace.com plenty, though. I saved his files on a CD-ROM. Now that they're safely stored, I can use my WipeDrive 5TM program to erase everything off the hard drive. That way the college won't be able to use any of the information against the Clarks if they decide to sue."

"Do it," Rex said. "It's a bit late for the college to be intervening now. They had their chance to close down the site before it all ended in tragedy. How long will it take?"

"I'm doing it now."

"Make sure you leave everything in the room exactly the way you found it."

"Don't worry. I even wore gloves to get through the vent."

"A real pro."

"Okay, the data's been deleted. I'm closing down. See you in a few minutes."

Rex, unable to bear the suspense, took a stroll down to the second floor to make sure the coast was clear. Aiding and abetting a break-in was the most illegal thing he had ever done. He had not so much as run a red light since he passed the Scottish bar exam. A few students paused in respectful silence in front of Dix's door. No one was ascending from the first floor. Rex hurried back upstairs without being seen.

"We're golden," Campbell exclaimed as he reappeared through the ceiling, head first.

Rex helped him onto his feet. "So you found your way okay," he said, replacing the grill.

"I memorized the plan before I set out and rolled out a string so I could find my way back." Campbell's face was flushed from exertion and excitement.

"You did grand, lad."

Campbell pulled a rope and a CD-ROM from under his sweat shirt, which he had tucked into his jeans, and removed his latex gloves.

"Where did you get those?"

"I use them for dissections."

"I should never have asked. Anything else of interest on the PC?"

"I skimmed his personal emails. There were some nasty ones from Kris accusing him of screwing on the side. She said he made her sick. Nice, huh?"

"I think she may have meant that literally. What was the date on those emails?"

"She sent them shortly before Spring Break."

"Anything else?"

"There was a draft email to Cormack that Dix hadn't sent yet, blasting him for favoritism and denying having posted the picture of Ms. Johnson. He threatened to complain to the dean if Cormack didn't put up his grade."

"Let's get this desk back into place," Rex said.

When the furniture was back to normal, Campbell stripped out of his clothes. "Do I have time for a shower before the memorial service?"

Rex glanced at his watch. "Aye, if you're quick."

He had brought a dark jacket and tie with him that morning. While he waited for Campbell, he made a list in his notebook of people left to question. The memorial service would provide an opportunity to have a word with some key players in Dixon's life.

"Why so glum?" Campbell asked upon re-entering the room.

"It's a right depressing case. I keep thinking, 'There but for the grace of God.'"

"Don't worry, Dad. I'm not going to go and do anything stupid. How do I look?"

"Verra nice."

Campbell did indeed look extremely handsome in his black slacks and ironed white shirt. His tall body made for an elegant clothes horse. He put on a pair of dress shoes over his black socks and applied gel to his hair, preening in the mirror inside the closet door. Rex was under no illusion as to whom his son was going to all this trouble for.

"We'll be late," he reminded Campbell, tapping his watch.

"Did you order the flowers?"

"A big purple wreath from the both of us," Rex said as they left the room and strode down the corridor. "Do you have the address of the church?"

"I know where it is. It's not far."

"You drive while I put on my tie."

As they reached the parking lot, Rex felt hollow. Memorial services made him more uneasy than hospitals. The April sky was overcast, threatening rain, in sympathetic mourning for the twenty-year-old boy from Nantucket.

FOURTEEN

THE PAIRED, NARROW-ARCHED WINDOWS of the Gothic Revival church were paned with stained glass, indenting the smooth beige façade. A group of people stood on the steps beneath the red-tiled porch roof. Rex saw Campbell's gaze lock onto Melodie, who was in conversation with her parents. She wore a simple black dress and diamond drop earrings, looking the very picture of decorum and class. Kris Florek entered the church with Mike, the business major from Indiana. Rex looked around for the other students he had met. Red and Justin mingled with their peers on the lawn. The mood was somber.

Shortly afterward, Dr. Binkley, cloaked in his black gown, arrived on a bicycle. "Isn't that the dean of students?" Rex asked Campbell.

"He lives on the campus perimeter and bikes pretty much everywhere."

Members of the faculty joined the dean as he strode up the path. Campbell greeted Mrs. Clark with a hug and a kiss on the cheek and received a warm handshake from her husband. While Campbell said hello to Melodie, Rex took the parents aside and informed them he was making progress in the case, without divulging that he was now almost convinced their son's death was a murder. He wanted actual proof before dropping the bombshell. That Dixon had not downloaded the suicide instructions, at least not from his own computer, was not enough evidence.

Removing the CD-ROM from his pocket, he told them that Campbell had saved the data from Dixon's PC. "If you give me permission to look at it, I can then forward it to you, unless you'd rather have it now."

"It's too painful right now," Katherine said. "But please send it on when you're done with it."

The church bell rang in the tower, and people started moving toward the entrance. The Clarks invited him and Campbell to sit with them, but Rex declined, saying he preferred to observe from the back. He detained his son before he could follow Melodie down the central aisle as organ music burst from the chancel.

"Who's that lad behind us?" he asked in a fierce whisper, recognizing the boy who had sworn a lot and tried to break down Dixon's door on Sunday night.

"Klepto," his son replied. "Dix's ex-roommie."

"Good, I wanted a word with him." Rex had imagined Klepto as a furtive-looking individual, but this boy was of average build and sauntered confidently up the path, hands thrust into the slit pockets of a brushed leather jacket.

"See you later," Campbell said, hurrying after Melodie.

Rex buttonholed Klepto before he could step through the door. "I remember you from Sunday night," he said, guiding him back into the emptying vestibule. "Sorry—I didn't get your name."

"Ty Clapham. I go by Klepto."

"That's a bit of an unfortunate nickname, isn't it? Or is it well deserved?"

The slim-fitting zippered jacket featured an array of pockets, perhaps useful for hiding items. Rex could not help but wonder how Klepto had come by such an expensive article of clothing.

"Do I steal, d'you mean? I prefer to call it appropriation of assets. You have no idea how careless some of these kids are with their stuff. I'm not a kleptomaniac in the clinical sense. I do what I do for material gain, not because of a morbid condition."

"I'm glad to hear it," Rex said curtly. "Ever been in trouble with the law?"

"Never."

"Perhaps 'not yet' would be a better answer. And, remember, kleptomania is not generally accepted as an affirmative defense. I understand you were Dixon's roommate last year?"

"That's right." The boy made direct eye contact. "What's with all the questions?"

"I'm looking out for Dixon's interests. The Clarks are nice people. I said I would try to find out more about the circumstances surrounding their son's death."

Through the door, Rex could see that the sanctuary had filled up to almost full capacity. A minister began speaking at the flower-laden altar, too far away to be audible.

"Did you write that ditty on StudentSpace.com—the one about the man from Nantucket?"

"I'm a psych major, not an f-ing poet."

"It's not much of a poem. I noticed that you seem to have a predilection for the f-word, which appears in the ditty, interestingly enough."

"The word has gained wide currency in our illiterate society."

"You seem far from illiterate yourself, except for your overuse of the expletive."

"It's a verbal tick. My dissertation's going to be about vocal mannerisms and how they can reveal as much about a person as facial expressions."

They were way off topic. Rex was sure the psych major was messing with his head. "About the ditty…"

"Dix was my friend, so why would I post a nasty poem?"

"Why indeed? I'm simply trying to arrive at the truth. Isn't that what psychology is all about?"

"To paraphrase: The truth is rarely pure and never simple. Actually, psychology has more to do with perception."

"For someone who claims not to be a poet, it's a wee bit surprising you can quote Oscar Wilde."

"Just because someone can quote someone else, doesn't make them a poet."

Rex realized he was not going to be able to flatter any information out of Klepto. The boy was too astute. "You know something, don't you?" he said.

"What makes you think that?"

"Because you're beating around the bush. There's something you want to say, but you're not sure I'm the person to tell."

For the first time in the conversation, a flicker crossed Klepto's inscrutable gray eyes. Rex knew he was right.

"Spit it out, lad. Or we can speak after the service, if you'd rather."

Klepto reached into an inside zip pocket and extracted a button, which he held up to Rex. "This is a button off R.J. Wylie's hoodie. I thought it might be a vital clue in Dix Clark's death."

"Where did you find it?"

"By Dix's chair the night he was found hanged. I saw it lying there after you broke down the door. While everyone was watching you get him down from the rope, I bent down to tie the lace on my sneaker and swiped it off the rug."

Rex stared at him. "Why did you take it?"

"I thought I might be able to use it."

"That's called obstruction of justice."

Klepto looked like he didn't care.

"Did you try and blackmail R.J. with it?"

"What if I did?"

"It wasn't a cool evening that night. I was wearing a short-sleeve shirt. Why would R.J. be wearing a hoodie?"

"To hide his face when he entered the main entrance to the resident hall."

"Do you mind if I hold onto this for the time being?" Rex asked, plucking the button from the boy's fingers. "Ta very much. How do you know it's his?"

"You'll find it matches his hoodie."

Rex thought this over for a moment. "We'd better go in now so we don't miss any more of the service," he murmured.

He took up position just inside the door, while Klepto slipped into a pew at the back. The minister was coming to the end of verse 3 of Isaiah 61: "… that they might be called trees of righteousness, the planting of the Lord, that he might be glorified." Rex drifted off in thought as he fixed his eyes on the floral arrangements and only came to again when he heard the opening words to his favorite psalm, "The Lord is my Shepherd." He bent his head and recited the soothing passage to himself. Psalm 23 had been read at his father's funeral when he was just seven years old. It was the part of the service he remembered most clearly.

The deacon took the minister's place for the Gospel reading. "I am the Resurrection and the Life … and whosoever believeth in Me shall never die."

Next, the haunting melody of "Angel" by Sarah McLaughlin floated down from the speakers, followed by a speech from the dean of students lamenting the all-too-short life of Dixon Clark, and how he would be sadly missed by students and faculty members alike. Justin, as captain of the soccer team and a co-member of the deceased's fraternity, stood up and said a few words. Another boy nervously delivered a series of anecdotes to the assembly, which laughed with polite restraint.

When the service was over, Rex stood by the entrance and watched as the mourners filed out of the church. Kris and Mike left together. The Clarks received condolences from staff members, among them Astra Knowles, the school registrar, dressed in a garment resembling a black tent.

"I'm getting something to eat with Melodie and her parents before they leave for the airport," Campbell said, approaching his father, hands plunged into the pockets of his dress pants. "Are you coming?"

"Thanks, but no. There are still a few people I want to talk to."

Campbell gave him the keys to the SUV. "I'll meet you back at the dorm around six-thirty."

Mr. Clark came over to shake his hand, while Katherine and Melodie waved from where they stood talking to the dean beneath the shade of a sabal palm.

"Take care," Keith told Rex.

"You too. It was a fine service. I liked the song about spending all your time waiting for that second chance."

"Kris chose it. It was one of Dix's favorites. In fact, Katherine and I have been talking. We've decided to set up a scholarship in Dix's name so we can help a deserving kid in his place. It might help make some sense out of all this."

Rex shook Keith's hand again in both of his. "That's a grand gesture. I'll be in touch."

He gazed after the family as they walked with his son to the rental car. The scene gave Rex a strange sense of premonition. But for Dixon's death, Campbell and Melodie might never have met.

FIFTEEN

THE DEAN WAS STOOPED over his bike twirling the combination on his lock when Rex joined him in the church parking lot.

"Dr. Binkley," he announced. "I'm Rex Graves. My son is a sophomore at Hilliard."

"Pleased to meet you." They shook hands. "That's a Scottish accent, isn't it? I did my PhD at the London School of Economics and visited Edinburgh many times. It's a fascinating city. What do you do there?"

"I prosecute in the High Court of Justiciary," Rex said, putting himself on an equal professional footing with the dean. The High Court was the supreme criminal court of Scotland and he had been appointed Queen's Counsel.

"Your son must be one of our foreign exchange students. What is he studying?"

"Marine science."

"An excellent program. The St. Johns River, its estuaries, and the Atlantic Ocean provide a plethora of marine habitats for study.

The *Calypso*, our twenty-five-foot Boston Whaler, facilitates field work for our students."

Rex already knew all this. The dean's barrage of words reminded him of his interview with the affable and voluble school registrar, Astra Knowles. "Actually, I wanted to talk to you about Dixon Clark. That was a moving eulogy you gave."

The dean shook his head sorrowfully. "It's a terrible thing to have a student die on your watch, as it were."

"I understand there was some ill-feeling between Dixon and another undergraduate by the name of R.J. Wylie."

"Are you going to pressure me to shut down the website too? I was just speaking to Mrs. Clark about it. She's threatening to sue the school for failing to comply with her son's request to shut it down. You're a lawyer. Do you think she has a case?"

"There may be grounds for a wrongful death suit if it can be proved the college took insufficient steps to prevent a suicide." Of course, this was all hypothetical, since Rex was not sure a suicide had occurred after all, but he felt it could do no harm for the dean to reconsider his position.

"We did ask the site to desist from posting inflammatory material," Dr. Binkley said, in the college's defense.

"Did you receive a response?"

"Only an email to the effect that StudentSpace.com is a personal website and students have a First Amendment right to free speech and expression."

"Have you consulted with an attorney?"

"We have."

That might explain the confiscation of Dixon's PC. "Addition-ally, the question of why campus security took so long to respond to the crisis might come up," Rex insinuated.

The dean's eyes narrowed behind his glasses. "Are you acting for the Clarks?"

"I am not acting in a legal capacity for anyone," Rex replied truthfully, while evading the question of his involvement with Mr. and Mrs. Clark. "I'm just curious as to why the other boy was expelled. This seems to be at the heart of the website controversy."

"The disciplinary board voted three to five not to reinstate Wylie."

"Why was that, if he was acquitted by a court of law?"

"We believed he was a bad influence. Several students testified that Wylie was using recreational drugs on campus."

"Were these witnesses credible?" The inference was that Dixon's own testimony had not proved to be so. The prosecution had failed to convince the jury that the dealer in the video was R.J. Wylie, who, in any case, had been signed in at a lab when the drug transaction took place.

Binkley bent down to attach bicycle clips to the pants of his suit. "Good to meet you, Mr. Graves," he said getting on his bike. "Hope we get the opportunity to talk again." With that, he pushed off on his pedal and sailed across the parking lot, the tails of his gown floating behind him as he greeted students in passing.

Rex stared after him, wondering just how many emails Dixon had sent the college begging them to take action. Hilliard had done no more than dispatch a civil email into cyberspace in response, to which StudentSpace.com had replied anonymously. Sighing, Rex got in the SUV. He had lost sight of Astra Knowles. It was doubtful she would return to the college office after 5:00.

He shrugged off his jacket and took out the button Klepto had given him. If the psychology student had tried to blackmail Wylie, he must know where he lived. Rex kicked himself for not having found out at the time, but he had not wanted to keep Dixon's ex-roommate from the service. Now Klepto was nowhere to be seen either.

As Rex turned onto the campus, he spied Cormack in front of the administrative building. The math professor was opening the door of a green Saturn for a shapely blonde whom Rex recognized from the website as Campbell's marine science professor. He swung into the space next to Cormack's car and climbed out of the SUV. The professor did not look pleased to see him, or maybe he just felt guilty for not attending the memorial service. Rex's formal tie attested to the fact that he had.

"Sorry to accost you like this, Mr. Cormack," he said. "But I wonder if you can tell me where I can find R.J. Wylie."

Cormack looked surprised, but did not ask the reason for the question. His companion had ducked into the passenger seat out of sight.

"Uh, let me see." The professor scratched his head. "He's from Florida. Fort Myers—that's it. Dunbar High has a strong math department and I've gotten a few students from there. R.J. had a natural gift for math." He seemed genuinely peeved that he had lost a good student.

"I remember you saying."

"I wasn't at the service," Cormack volunteered, "because Dixon Clark fabricated testimony against Wylie. Whoever dubbed him

'The Snitch' on StudentSpace.com called it right. And that's not all." He bent down and Rex heard the clink of car keys. "Put the air on. I won't be long," he told his passenger, closing the door. "Clark transposed Bethany's head onto a porn star's body." He glanced at the Saturn, leading Rex to understand that Bethany was the woman in the car.

"My son showed me. Ms. Johnson is his marine science professor."

"It's a scandal."

"Do you know who runs the site?"

"If I did, don't you think I'd murder the little shit?"

"I don't think Dixon was responsible for that picture. From what I understand, he was not very proficient in computer science. And from what I've met of his friends, I don't think they are either."

"Don't underestimate them. They don't have what we might call academic smarts, but if there was a way to distil beer from their oatmeal, they'd find it."

"Mrs. Clark has spoken to the dean about shutting down the site."

"Good," Cormack said between his teeth. "We wouldn't want another death on our hands."

Yanking open his door, he got in his car and reversed in a reckless curve. Rex watched him race out of the parking lot, reflecting that it must take a lot of emotion to turn a mathematician into a hot head. Still, from the quick glimpse he had caught of the girlfriend, he could understand Al Cormack's reaction.

SIXTEEN

REX WENT TO THE bagel shop for a coffee before returning to Campbell's room, where his son joined him a quarter of an hour later, looking subdued.

"How did it go with the Clarks?" Rex asked.

"It was nice. I don't know when I'll see Melodie again."

"Why don't you send her a postcard from the Keys?" Rex said, hoping they could still make it. A lot depended on wrapping up the case and getting Moira on the plane the next day. Campbell's face cleared at the suggestion. "I could send her some pictures of myself on the boat."

"There you go. But right now I need your help."

"What do you want me to do?"

"I'd like you to Google Dunbar High School in Fort Myers. I need a location so I can narrow my search."

"Who's in Fort Myers?" Campbell asked, taking the desk chair while Rex propped himself against the pillows on the bed.

"R.J. Wylie went to school there. If he's back home, I might be able to find him. Ray Junior's father must be called Ray. I'm hoping he'll be listed in the phone book."

"What are you going to say to him?"

"I'll play it by ear. What do I call for directory service in the States?"

"4-1-1." Campbell gave him the address of the school in Fort Myers.

The operator came back with five numbers for R. Wylie listings in the area. "One of them is for Ray Wylie Pool & Patio Service," she informed him.

"Thanks." Rex glanced up at Campbell.

"Could you see if you can dig up anything further of interest on the CD-ROM of Dixon's files while I check out these numbers? I'll try the pool company first. Perhaps it's a private number."

"He-llo," a nasal male voice answered. The canned laughter of a TV sitcom played in the background.

"Ray Wylie?"

"What can I do you for?"

"I wanted to speak to your son R.J."

"He's not here." Bingo! How many Ray Wylies with sons by the name of R.J. could there be? "He's up in Jax. Is this about a job?"

"It's more of a social call. My son knows him from college."

The man sighed heavily. "He don't got many friends left from Hilliard, 'cept for the boy he went to high school with. Ain't got a cell phone neither, but he works for LTB Construction. I just got back from visiting him. They'll tell ya what construction site he's at. And just so you knows, my boy's a good kid and the school never proved nothing."

"So I gather. I hear he was a good student."

"He was heartbroken when they kicked him out. He's wanted to be a chemist since he first started helping me out with the pool business. In high school, he and his friend worked for me weekends and vacations. Ray liked testing the pool water and reading the ph level and all that good stuff. I been trying to get him to come into the business with me full time, but he ain't gave up on Hilliard, even though we got no more money for it. It got used up in his defense. My wife works two jobs to help pay off the second mortgage we took out on the house. R.J. sends money when he can."

"Thank you, Mr. Wylie," Rex said, ending the conversation. He felt uncomfortable prying information out of the man when his reasons for talking to R.J. were less friendly than he had intimated. "Do you recognize this button?" he asked Campbell, pulling it out of his pocket.

"No. I mean, it looks pretty generic."

"Apparently it belongs to a hoodie and was found next to Dixon's chair the night he died."

"Who found it?"

"Klepto."

"Figures."

"Why d'you say that?"

"Klepto finds everything that's lying around. How do you know it's not Dixon's?"

"I don't. I could email Mr. Clark, but I'd rather ask R.J. if it's his first. I need to talk to him anyway, but I suppose it'll have to wait until tomorrow, when he's at work."

"Did Klepto tell you it was R.J.'s?"

"Aye. R.J. is not responding to his blackmailing demands."

123

"That is so like Klepto," Campbell exclaimed in indignation. "Any way to make an easy buck. I heard he was sponging off an older woman, living at her house for free. He borrowed her Beamer once to attend an evening seminar. Mike saw it."

"Klepto does seem like a lovely character," Rex agreed. "Did you find anything on the CD-ROM?"

"A slew of emails going back to last semester, which he sent to various staff and faculty at Hilliard, complaining about the website."

"Let's forward those to Keith Clark."

"In an email to Dr. Binkley's secretary, he said he had proof of who was running SS.com."

"See if you can find out who it was."

Campbell busily typed away for a few minutes. "The domain name is registered to a Luella Shaw."

"Is that a fictitious name?"

"Could be. All the girls I know on campus are called Ashley, Brittany, or Kristin."

"Is there a telephone number or address listed?"

"999-999-9999. That's certainly fictitious. The address given is Florida 32211, which is this zip code. Nothing else. The domain registration company operates out of Belize."

"Sounds a bit fly-by-night."

"Are we going out for dinner?" Campbell asked.

"I thought you already ate with the Clarks."

"Yeah, but that was just a snack at some posh tea shop."

"I have to see Moira, but if you want to wait in the car, we can go to that beachfront restaurant afterwards."

"How long will you be?"

"No more than an hour."

Campbell pulled an undecided face.

"You could use the time to study. I'll need you to come with me tomorrow to take her to the airport, in case she pulls another stunt. We'll be leaving early, so it would be better if you spent the night at the motel." In any case, now that Rex was almost convinced Dixon had been murdered, he didn't like the idea of Campbell staying in the dorm before the killer was found.

"Okay." Campbell slid his laptop into his computer bag and grabbed a few items of clothing, which he stuffed in a hold-all.

"By the way, I liked what you wrote about Earth being a living, breathing organism creating oceans and continents. It sounded like you were describing God."

"Did it? I only meant to make an analogy with humans." Campbell smiled warmly. "But I'm glad you liked it."

They left the room and drove to the hospital where Rex found a shaded parking spot. The sun burned low in the sky in a fierce final effort before it set.

"Are you coming in?" he asked.

"I'll stay here. Hospitals depress me."

Rex took Moira's suitcase from the backseat and proceeded to her floor. As he passed the nurses' station, Dr. Yee smiled briskly and formed an 'O' with her thumb and forefinger. *That must mean we're on for tomorrow*, Rex said to himself. *Hallelujah*. He would breathe a mighty sigh of relief once Moira was on the plane headed home.

"Oh, good, you brought my suitcase," she exclaimed as he entered her room. "Pass it here, would you?" She extracted a compact from her sponge bag and proceeded to powder her nose and apply lipstick. The bandages on her wrists had been replaced with adhesive strips. "I was wondering if I'd see you today."

Rex perched on the side of her bed. "I've been really busy and canna stay long. Campbell's waiting in the car."

"You should have brought him up to see me."

"He's studying."

"A likely excuse. He never was one for studying."

"You'd be surprised," Rex said, curbing his irritation. Moira had no right to criticize his son. She had no rights on him at all now that they were no longer dating. "He doesn't like hospitals. I suppose it reminds him of when he visited his mother when she was dying of cancer. You'll see him tomorrow, though. He's coming to the airport with us."

A corner of Moira's lip twitched. "A grand trip it's been for me! One walk along the beach and the rest of the time in hospital."

"Come on, Moira. You brought it on yourself. Coming to the States, I mean."

"I suppose so." She zipped the sponge bag. "How are you getting on with the case?"

"I'll know more tomorrow, but I believe the lad was murdered."

"Murdered?" Moira's eyes widened with interest. "Who killed him?"

"There are a bunch of people with enough motive."

"You can tell me. It's not like I know anyone here, so I'm not going to go telling anyone."

"One of his professors didn't like him, for starters. He thinks the lad got his best student expelled unjustly from the university. He's also got it into his head that the victim posted a nude photo of his girlfriend on a student website. From everything I know about the deceased, which admittedly isn't much, I don't think he was responsible for the picture. For one thing, he comes from a nice family. I just don't see him doing something like that. But then I don't see him framing the wrong boy for a crime either."

"Who else is on your list of suspects? I'd like to take a guess. Then you can tell me if I'm right when you find out."

Since the "game" seemed to amuse her, Rex continued his review of the case. "The professor's girlfriend herself could have done it, but there's the problem of getting into the boy's room. The killer must have climbed in through a vent in the ceiling. Only the occupant of the above room or someone close to him would likely have known about it."

"Or an engineer possibly. Who is the occupant?"

"Currently Campbell. Last year it belonged to a student called R.J., the math professor's pet."

"You don't need to use initials. I told you—I'm no blabbermouth."

"That's the name he goes by. It's short for Ray Junior. I hope to see him tomorrow. Another boy gave me a button off R.J.'s fleece that he said he found at the scene of the hanging. R.J. is the one who got expelled."

"My guess is R.J. murdered the boy out of revenge."

"Wait. There's also the victim's girlfriend, a student called Kris. They had a big row before he went home for Easter. She thinks he was cheating on her. Also, it's university policy to grant a passing grade to those closest to the person who died, and it seems she was failing her nursing degree."

"It's her then. She would know about how best to kill someone. And maybe he gave her the key or code to his room so she could get in when she liked."

Rex shook his head. "She saw him hanging from the ceiling fan through the doorframe. She was unable to get in."

"Maybe she just pretended not to have her key on her, to give him enough time to die. Hangings usually take only minutes. She'd know that if she's training to be a nurse. Once you stop breathing, there's no oxygen to the brain and you become unconscious. I heard it was one of the least painful ways to die."

"I hope so for the boy's sake, but not as instantaneous as fracturing your neck from a long drop." He studied Moira's face. "Promise me you won't try anything like this again. It's painful for the people left behind." And selfish, he thought.

"It just seemed like the best solution. When I took the Tylenol PM you gave me, I thought how wonderful it would be never to wake up. But I did wake up, very early, still feeling depressed. That's when I got your razor."

Rex hung his head with a sigh. "Moira."

"Tell me about the other suspects."

"Well, there are people who took sides with R.J. His expulsion caused something of a furor on a student website. A random killer wouldn't have known how to get into the victim's room. So the murderer had to make it look like a suicide. Nothing was stolen as far as I know. His parents packed up the contents of his room and never mentioned that anything had gone missing, except for a silk tie."

"But a button mysteriously turned up."

"Aye, the button."

"It's very creepy."

"Premeditated murders are always creepy. So," Rex said. "What's your final verdict?"

"It could be any one of the people you mentioned."

"Very helpful. Anyway, I'll see you early in the morning. Dr. Yee will be on duty. I'll go and settle up now to save time."

The medical bill came as a shock. "Just as well I'm in a hospital," he told the clerk at the payment office. "The bill is enough to give me a heart attack."

The cashier gave him an agreement to sign whereby the hospital could charge his Visa card if further costs were incurred before Moira left. Further costs! Not that he didn't have adequate funds. However, he was in the process of converting a hunting lodge in the Highlands and it was costing him a bundle. He thought it would be grand to spend time there with Helen, although he hadn't told her about it yet. It was going to be a surprise.

As he crossed the main lobby of the hospital, he was appalled to see an automated teller machine. The National Health Service in Britain might leave something to be desired, but he was grateful for it all the same.

"Why the frown?" Campbell asked when Rex climbed into the driver's seat of the Trailblazer.

"Moira doesn't have traveller's insurance, and I'm not sure it would have covered a suicide attempt anyway."

"You didn't pay her hospital bill, did you?"

Rex reversed out of the parking space. "She doesn't earn a lot from her job and I feel responsible in a way. I never gave her the time of day when she came to see me in Edinburgh."

"Yeah, but still. And you say Consuela is high maintenance."

Rex smiled wryly. "*Touché.*"

He experienced an acute craving for his pipe, which was strange, since he had not smoked much since arriving in Florida. The hot weather was not conducive to smoking. He felt on edge, his nerves in suspense, whether more from the effort of dealing with Moira or the pressure of solving the murder in time, he could not be sure.

SEVENTEEN

"How are you bearing up?" Rex asked Moira as he carried her suitcase across the hospital parking lot. The sun was rising in a sky of rippled amber—a scene he would have preferred to enjoy from his ocean-view balcony over a leisurely cup of coffee.

She meekly held onto his arm, taking small steps. "They never let you sleep in hospital. At four this morning, an orderly came in to deliver clean towels. Or maybe it's just so they can keep an eye on you."

"You'll be able to sleep on the plane."

"Do we have time to get breakfast?"

"We'll get some at the airport. I don't know how long it'll take to get there."

Although Jacksonville was even bigger than Miami and had its own system of freeways soaring into concrete loops around the city, Rex found it easier to navigate. All the same, he didn't want to risk the catastrophic consequences of Moira missing her flight.

Campbell dozed in the back seat as they sped up I-95 to the airport among a sprinkling of freight trucks and early commuters.

"You can tell me all about progress in the case," Moira said. "I'm about to get on the plane, so I won't be able to leak any information."

"All right." More relaxed now that they were well on their way, Rex quickly organized his thoughts. "The case against R.J., according to newspaper stories, was based on the word of a career criminal and paid informant of the Jacksonville Police Department and on corroboration by Dixon Clark, who as a resident assistant was supposed to report any suspicious drug activity in the dorms." He had read up on the case from various newspaper articles online.

"Dixon Clark being the boy found dead in his room?"

"Correct. The informant told the police he'd purchased cocaine from R.J. twice, but university records show R.J. was in the lab on the other side of campus when the buys took place. Dixon secretly videoed one of the transactions, but the recording proved too blurry to serve as conclusive evidence, and R.J. was acquitted. However, the university's disciplinary board voted not to reinstate him because they believed Dixon."

"I still think R.J. did it."

"Everything seems to point that way. When I discovered that his room, now Campbell's, was directly above Dixon's, I thought I might well be dealing with a case of murder rather than suicide. By tracking Dixon's Internet activities, Campbell was able to confirm there was no indication the deceased ever surfed the suicide website from which a set of how-to instructions were downloaded and left on his desk."

When Rex realized he had mentioned suicide, he glanced over at Moira. She was staring out her window, a lost expression on her face.

"We're making good time," he remarked with false cheer. "We can get your baggage checked in and then see about breakfast."

"I'll take my case with me as carry-on, otherwise it might get lost. And I want to get some duty free."

Rex hoped she wasn't going to buy liquor. He wasn't sure when she had started drinking, unless Monday night had been a one-off.

"I'm sorry about what happened," she blurted, as though reading his thoughts. "I had a lot of time to think in hospital. You're not to blame."

"The important thing is that you get yourself better. Heather will take good care of you."

"But what about afterwards?"

"Won't you continue with your work?"

"I suppose."

Rex patted the small hands clasped limply in her lap. "You've been through a lot."

He followed the signs to the Continental terminal and woke Campbell up. "Can you park the car while we queue up at the ticket counter?"

Afterward, Rex called Campbell on his cell to tell him where they would be having breakfast. Moira ordered the special. Rex restricted himself to a coffee and Danish. The coffee was weak and tasted as though it had been left stewing for hours.

"They don't care," Moira remarked, pushing hers aside. "They won't see most of their customers again."

"The best airport coffee I ever had was in Paris."

"They're serious about their food in France. The French would never put up with this pigswill. Using that word would be a grievous insult in a Muslim country, you know. You have to be very careful."

Campbell joined them and ordered a Coke and waffles.

"The breakfast of champs," Rex remarked.

"So, Moira, are you looking forward to being back in Scotland?" his son asked. "I'll bet it's raining over there."

Rex kicked him under the table. "Moira will take the sunny weather back home with her."

"You'd never think I'd been in Florida," she said, contemplating her pale hands.

"Och, you never did tan all that much," Rex said.

"Anyway, the sun gives you wrinkles," Campbell added, catching on. "You wouldn't want that."

Moira asked how he was getting on with his studies and what he did in his free time, and Rex was glad to see him make an effort to be sociable, even though he knew how his son felt about her. The strain of waiting for her to finally be off made Rex feel like a ticking time bomb. He would explode if the flight was delayed.

With less than an hour left to board, Rex escorted her to the security checkpoint and hugged her goodbye. Dry-eyed, she bid him a curt farewell. He lingered while she went up to the X-ray machine and placed her handbag and shoes in a plastic tray and her small suitcase on the conveyor belt. As she was about to walk through the metal detector, he turned away with a final wave and heard the alarm go off.

"No-o-o-o," screamed a voice in his head. He looked back in panic. An armed female guard, taking Moira aside, waved a wand down her back and up the inside of her spread legs. It buzzed when it reached chest level. Rex watched in shock as the guard directed Moira to lift her blouse. The passengers awaiting their turn fell silent and stared. A second guard approached Moira with his hand on his holster. She turned in desperation to Rex, who pushed his way through the line. A guard blew a whistle.

"You can't treat her like that!" Rex protested over the heads of waiting passengers.

"We're on high alert. We're looking for a female terrorist fitting this woman's description. Step back!"

"She's no terrorist!"

"I'll need to see your passport," the guard told Moira.

Retrieving her handbag, she stretched out her arm to deliver the document. The guard bristled when he saw her bandaged wrist.

"You were in Iraq?" he questioned when he came to the stamped entry. "You'll have to come with me."

"Her underwire bra set off the alarm," the female guard informed him.

"Let her through," Rex pleaded, wondering when she had started wearing underwire bras. Weren't those what Victoria's Secret models wore to enhance their bust line? "She belongs to a church group, which goes to trouble spots all over the world! She's not a threat. I can vouch for her. I'm a member of the Scottish bar."

"You can go," the guard told her, regarding Rex as though he couldn't care less about his legal credentials.

Moira reclaimed her suitcase and shoes, and made for the departure lounge without so much as a backward glance. Rex watched her disappear down the concourse. His knees wobbled with the giddy realization that she was out of his life—for now, at least, though he could not help but feel desperately sorry for her.

Grabbing Campbell by the shoulder, he guided him toward the terminal exit. "Let's get out of here," he said, "before something else goes wrong."

EIGHTEEN

While Campbell drove, Rex called directory assistance and got the number for LTB Construction. The office manager told him where R.J. Wylie was working and gave him directions.

"I can chill at the Landing while you talk to R.J.," Campbell suggested.

Rex reached into his wallet and pulled out a fifty dollar bill. "Here you go. Get yourself something for the Keys."

"Thanks, Dad!"

They drove downtown in slow-moving traffic. At night, the blue-lit Main Street Bridge and illuminated skyscrapers cast ribbons of neon color across the river. Rex had taken a photo the last time he was in Jacksonville, though it hadn't done the scene justice. This morning the glassy towers sparkled with sunlight above the marina. The Landing, a complex of bistros and boutiques built on the waterfront, successfully combined urban chic and Florida casual. They entered Bay Street across from the Modis Building and parked the SUV.

"I'll call you," Rex said as they split into different directions.

As he approached the LTB construction site, a bronze glass skyscraper with scaffolding scaling one side loomed over him, dwarfing the tall buildings around it. A giant crane stood motionless against the azure sky. Within the wire fence lay piles of concrete blocks and stacks of pipes. Rex opened the gate and made his way to the trailer. Before he had taken two steps across the yard, a robust man in a yellow construction vest waved his arms at him.

"Hey! You there!" he shouted. "This is a hard hat area. You need to get outta here."

"I'm looking for R.J. Wylie."

"He's up there somewhere. I'm his super. What d'you want him for?"

"Can you tell him his dad told me where I could find him? It's important."

The man radioed up to the tower. "He'll be down in the cherry picker in just a minute," he told Rex. "He's a good kid. Comes to work on time, does what he's told. But you'll have to wait outside the gate."

Minutes later, a mechanical arm lowered a red steel basket to the ground. A young man in jeans, yellow vest, and a white T-shirt and hat stepped out. The supervisor pointed to the gate where Rex waited, and he nodded. He was about Campbell's height with more developed shoulders and a broader chest.

"I'm R.J.," he said opening the gate. "The boss said you wanted a word."

"I wanted to discuss what happened last year when you were suspended from Hilliard."

"You must be the Scottish boy's dad. You sound just like him. Whose side are you on?" Hazel eyes fringed with thick black lashes gazed at him in curiosity from a well-formed face edged with dark stubble. A silver ring pierced his right ear.

"The Dixons asked me to look into their son's suicide, but I'm not taking sides. I'm just trying to get at an approximation of the truth."

"My expulsion was a crock. The dean of students was just looking for a way to get rid of me."

"Why would he do that?"

"I strung his bicycle up on a tree last year. It was an April Fool's dare—a prank. That's the real reason Bikey-Bink was pissed at me."

"Did you sell drugs?"

"Sell? No! I handed a bit out when I had some to spare. Pot mostly, including to your son."

"Campbell?"

"Sure. Just the one time. Don't worry, he's not a pothead, far as I know."

Rex took a moment to recover from this revelation.

"Look, it wasn't me on the tape. Any moron could see that. The gray hoodie didn't even look like mine. But the cops needed to make a bust. Their informant was making $60 off them for every buy he reported. Thing is, he never bought from me. I never dealt. Period."

Rex held up the button that Klepto had given him.

R.J. pulled a cigarette and lighter from his jeans pocket. "Not mine. Lots of students have hoodies. Anyway, school records prove I was in the chem. lab at the time the bust went down. I couldn't have been in two places at once. Plus my lawyer pointed out in court that the guy in the video standing next to the informant, a man of six foot, was inches shorter. I'm six-two. You couldn't even see a face under the hood. It took less than thirty minutes of deliberation for the jury to deliver a verdict of not guilty."

"Who arrested you?"

"Campus Security. Then Detective Beecham came to question me and took me to the station for no good reason other than I couldn't produce the hoodie I was supposedly wearing. I told him it wasn't me on the video, and he said he had a list of six eye-witnesses who confirmed I had the exact same hoodie. At first I said I didn't need a lawyer because I hadn't done what they accused me of. He and his partner questioned me for four hours straight. They found a second person to say he'd bought from me. I never saw either man in my life."

R.J. kicked at the dirt with the toe of his work boot. "Not that it would make a difference now, but I could prove that button doesn't come from my hoodie."

"This isna aboot the drug bust. It was allegedly found in Dixon's room the night he died."

"So?"

"I don't think his death was a suicide."

R.J.'s face blanched. "Shit … Excuse me, but what are you saying, sir?"

"Someone got to Dixon from your old room."

"How?"

"A system of air ducts leads to his room."

"I don't have access to my old room. If I as much as set foot on school grounds, campus security would arrest me."

"A hoodie would disguise your face. Like you said, several students have ones that are similar."

R.J.'s face tightened in rage. "I better not be getting the rap for murder as well as dealing. Why me? Lots of kids experiment with drugs. Why did Dix single me out? And why the fuck are you looking at me for his murder?"

"You have a compelling motive for killing him. He got you kicked out of Hilliard. You could have gone to prison for dealing."

"Yeah, I could. He totally ruined my life."

"You ruined it the day you first took drugs. *You* blew your degree at Hilliard."

R.J. clamped his arms across his chest and stared off into the middle distance. "Don't I know it! Not a day goes by when I don't kick myself. But I'm clean now, six months. I even volunteer in a mentor program teaching kids about the risks of drugs. Whatever; I didn't kill Dix Clark."

Rex glanced over the barrier. "You work in construction. You'd know all about air ducts."

"If I'm gonna get framed again for something I never did, I'd rather end it now." R.J. chucked his cigarette butt on the ground. "I haven't got any money left for a defense. And that bitch never even stood by me."

Before Rex could understand what was happening, R.J. swung open the gate and sprinted across the job site. Enclosed in a construction elevator, he rose up the glass façade of the building.

"Where's he going?" Rex asked the super who stopped him as he chased after the boy.

"To the top. What did you say to him?"

"He's been implicated in a murder."

"Christ, as if that kid hasn't been through enough trouble already." The super tilted back his head and followed the elevator's progress to the dizzying bronze pinnacle of the skyscraper. He got on his radio. "Pete, R.J.'s on your floor. He may be suicidal. Don't approach. I'm comin' up."

"I'm coming with you," Rex said.

"Grab a hat from the trailer."

Rex found one on a hook inside the door and joined the super who led him around the building to a second elevator.

"You should be wearing a harness," the supervisor said, hesitating as they stepped onto the platform. At close quarters, he reeked of Marlboroughs.

"No time. Beam me up, Scotty."

The super set the hydraulic lift in motion. "Name's Tony," he said thrusting a calloused hand into Rex's. "Hope you're not scared of heights. That hat's not gonna do nothin' for you if you fall from the sixtieth floor."

Rex was not prone to acrophobia, but he had never ridden in an outdoor elevator. As a precaution, he decided not to look down. "Do you test employees for drugs?" he asked, trying to gauge R.J.'s state of mind.

"It's mandatory at LTB."

Perhaps R.J. was telling the truth about being clean. The floors sped down to meet them, reflecting the mesh cage off the bronze panes. Toward the summit, Rex's ears popped. He did not venture a peek until he reached the top. From here the site looked like a sandbox littered with die-cast trucks and blocks of Lego. He fought down a reeling sense of nausea.

Tony let him out of the elevator and, clearing the other men off the roof and construction platform, led Rex across the concrete floor latticed with naked steel girders. The breeze, barely noticeable before, flattened Rex's shirt against his torso. R.J., standing perfectly still, was staring over the edge. He had removed his hard hat, and his dark hair blew about his forehead. Rex could not look at him without seeing the tops of surrounding towers spiking the skyline. If something happened to R.J., he would never forgive himself, especially if the boy was innocent.

"Come away from there, R.J.," he called. "I just want to talk to you."

"What's the point?" A gust buffeted the boy and he took a step to steady himself. Another step and he would go over the low rail and fall sixty floors. "I should have done this before and saved my parents the money for my defense. What good did it do?"

"I want to see justice is done."

Behind Rex, Tony murmured into his radio. "Call the cops. No sirens or lights."

"Just think what this would do to your parents," Rex reasoned with R.J. "One boy is already dead."

"I didn't kill him! I didn't!" R.J. stepped over the rail.

Rex's stomach completed a somersault. "I believe you! Klepto gave me the button."

"Should have known!" the boy cried out, looking back in despair. "But I could prove it's not mine."

"Come over here and tell me about it."

R.J. turned away and peered over the brink. This was the second where, in the recklessness of youth, he could decide to end his life and make a dramatic, poignant, and ultimately futile statement. Rex sprang forward just as the boy let himself fall head first in slow motion. Adrenalin pumped through his veins.

Grabbing him around the waist with one arm, Rex hooked a vertical beam with the other. The impact of R.J.'s weight pulled him forward, almost wrenching both arms from their sockets. A telescopic view of asphalt, cars and tree tops swam before his eyes before he managed to yank R.J. away from the edge, bringing him keeling on top of him as he hit concrete.

Tony pulled R.J. to his feet and stood gripping him by the shoulders. Rex lay for a moment staring at the sky. He had a fleeting notion that the world had gone mad. His heart reverberated through his body while concentric waves of pain shot through his elbow.

A construction worker helped him up. "I just saw the cops pull into the site," he told Tony.

A spasm of terror crossed R.J.'s face.

"Don't worry," Tony said. "We won't say nothing about this. Let's get off of this building. I got a first-aid kit in the trailer," he told Rex.

A cop approached them when they reached ground level.

"What's up, Tony?"

"Trailer got broke into again. Don't think anything went missing, but they jimmied the lock."

"Who's this?" the cop asked, looking at Rex.

"A building inspector. He fell and scraped his arm pretty bad. Lemme see to it first. Come with us," Tony instructed R.J., prodding Rex up the steps to the trailer.

They removed their hats and dumped them on the desk. Stale smoke hung in the stuffy air. Tony rummaged among a pile of rolled-up plans on a shelf and extracted a white plastic box marked with a red cross. He handed Rex a wad of cotton wool doused with hydrogen peroxide and a large Band-Aid.

"You can use that room back there if you guys need to talk. Here, take this." Tony gave R.J. a Thermos flask from off the desk. "It'll do you good. And take the rest of the day off. You wanna talk, call. I got to see to the cop and make a report on the break-in."

Rex, holding the wad to his bleeding elbow, made his way past the water cooler into a closed-off room equipped with a small desk and two chairs. He sat down and stuck the Band-Aid on his arm while R.J. took a seat and twisted off the lid to the scuffed flask. An aroma of sweetened coffee rose into the air. R.J. filled the cup and pushed the rest toward Rex, who took a swig straight from the Thermos. Though no longer burning hot, it tasted fresh and strong, much better than the coffee he had been served at the airport restaurant that morning.

"Tony's a good guy," R.J. remarked, speaking for the first time since his brush with death.

"Aye. He seems to think mighty highly of you too. You gave us quite a turn."

"You saved my life. That was a crazy thing you did, man. You could've gone over with me."

"I wouldna've let that happen. I have a strong sense of self-preservation."

R.J. ran a hand through his dark hair. "I can't explain what happened. All the time I was riding to the top, I thought I would never do it when it came right down to it. And then when I looked over, it all seemed so simple."

"I would never have forgiven myself if you'd gone over."

R.J. shrugged in response.

"How do you feel now?"

"Light-headed, I guess. Like nothing really matters, except that I can feel every pulse in my body. The coffee tastes better than anything I ever had before."

Rex guessed R.J. was feeling an adrenalin rush. As for himself, he was shaking. "My ex-girlfriend tried to commit suicide on Tuesday," he found himself confiding.

"You should carry a government health warning. Seems like people all around you are trying to self-destruct."

Rex smiled ruefully. "The doctor said it wasna a serious attempt, but still … It's a terrible thing to think about."

"I was thinking about someone in that moment before I let myself go. I remember saying to myself, 'Now she'll be sorry.' She could have saved me from having to go to court. All she had to do was go to the police and show them my hoodie, and tell them she had it all along."

"Why didn't she? Who is she?"

R.J. shook his head. "I can't tell you—I promised I'd never tell."

"And when did you make this promise?"

"When we were in my bed the first time. Just lying there whispering in the dark." R.J.'s voice caught in his throat. "I would have done anything for her."

"Did she feel the same way? If she did, why didn't she go to the police? Why didn't she try to protect you?"

R.J. hunched over the table. "Maybe she thought I'd never be convicted. Then, when I was expelled, she probably thought it was too late to come forward. I don't know if she ever spoke to the dean because by then she had stopped taking my calls."

"Would she have had any authority with him?"

"Probably not. Cormack didn't. And I know he tried."

"I could talk to the dean."

"The faculty would never admit to making a mistake. And Binkley would just argue I was using, which is against university policy."

"Can they actually prove you were using? My guess is they don't have much of a case, since the video failed to incriminate you."

"A couple of students testified that they saw me snort coke. I have no money for college now anyway. It'll take me years to pay off my defense."

Rex leaned forward. "Be that as it may, I need to be absolutely convinced of your innocence in Dixon's murder. You have to tell me about the button if it absolves you."

R.J. sat back in his chair. "I can't."

"Then I don't know how I can help you." Rex reached into his pocket and slid one of his business cards across the desk. "Here's my cell number. I'll be in town until tomorrow." He stood up and, on his way to the door, stopped by R.J.'s chair. He gave his shoulder a paternal squeeze, sighed heavily and left.

Tony was talking to the cop at the foot of the trailer steps. He escorted Rex to the gate. "Is he okay?"

"He's not very communicative."

"I'll keep an eye on him."

Rex took out his cell phone and called Campbell to tell him to meet him at the car.

"Can't we get lunch first?"

"Don't you have a lecture?"

"Not until two. How did it go with R.J.?"

"It was hair-raising. I'll tell you all about it, but I need to get to the campus right away." Rex remembered to look both ways before crossing the street. Sometimes he forgot that traffic moved in the opposite direction from home. He didn't want to have survived a close call on a skyscraper just to be hit by a car.

"There's someone I need to see immediately," he told Campbell over the phone. "Could be downright embarrassing if I'm wrong, but I have to give it a shot."

NINETEEN

Rex stopped by the Student Health Center where a nurse cleaned the cut on his elbow and applied a fresh dressing. By the time he reached the Marine Science Department, the pain in his arm had subsided to a throb. Students were spilling out of the building.

"Where can I find Professor Johnson?" he asked a coed.

"We just came out of her class. She's in the wet lab."

Rex entered a classroom set up with long work benches. A marker board covered most of the back wall. Other walls displayed fish mounts and enlarged checks granted by various organizations for marine research. But no sign of Ms. Johnson.

An adjoining lab contained a central fish tank. Through the open door, Rex glimpsed a collection of aquaria and microscopes lining the wall counters. The young assistant professor came out wearing a tight, ribbed sweater beneath her lab coat, her honey blond hair clasped in a ponytail. She could not be older than twenty-six.

"Hi," she said, clearly surprised to see him.

"We ran into each other yesterday in the parking lot," Rex reminded her, in case she had forgotten. "But we were not formally introduced." Cormack, the math professor, had all but pushed her into the car.

"You're Campbell's father. Nice kid. He writes beautiful reports. I guess British schools do a better job at teaching English."

"I'm afraid I'm not here to discuss Campbell's progress, although, naturally, I am always interested to hear how he's getting on. What I've come to discuss has nothing directly to do with my son."

Ms. Johnson leaned back against a workbench, hands gripping the edge, and held him in her blue gaze. She bore a passing resemblance to a young Brigitte Bardot. He hoped his hunch about her was right, otherwise he would merit a slap in the face.

"I've come about R.J. Wylie."

She blushed and looked away.

"Look, I'm not here to cause trouble. Whatever happened between you and R.J. is none of my business, except in-so-far as it relates to my investigation into Dixon Clark's death."

She started to say something, but stopped.

Rex stuck his hands into his pockets and paced between the benches, talking calmly as though delivering a lecture. "You borrowed his hoodie. It was cold that late October night or early morning when you crept out of the dorm. When he was arrested, the garment was still in your possession, so he could not prove that his jacket wasn't exactly the same as the one in the video. All the time he was in custody, he kept quiet because he didn't want to expose you and subject you to censure by the university. Am I on the right track so far?"

The young woman nodded, a troubled expression on her face. "I was a coward. Does Al know?"

"Cormack? Not through me. And not through R.J. That lad has a misplaced sense of loyalty, if you'll forgive me for saying so. He threw himself off a rather tall building this morning."

Bethany Johnson gasped, her hands flying to her mouth.

"He's all right physically. I caught him just in time. But I hope that gives you some idea of the pressure he's been under. He's working a dangerous construction job." Rex looked around the classroom. "He gave up his degree for you. If you had come forward at the beginning, the outcome might have been different."

He didn't care if he was being harsh on her. She made no effort to deny any of it, and here she was sitting pretty while her distraught young ex-lover had dangled over the side of a skyscraper.

"I was paying off student loans and living back at home. My parents would never have approved of the relationship," she said in her defense. "Then, when R.J. was arrested, I couldn't risk visiting him in jail and compromising my position."

Which compromising position in particular? Rex asked himself. *A Kama Sutra one?*

"He wasn't one of my students," she went on hurriedly, in response to his raised eyebrow. "We met off campus at a concert. At around the time he was arrested, I had started seeing Al Cormack."

"You didn't tell him about your affair?" *Obviously.* Professor Cormack was all about ethics.

"No. He was rooting for R.J. and fighting the university to get him re-admitted. I couldn't tell him."

I see trouble in paradise, Rex predicted, wondering if Cormack would waive his ethics in Ms. Johnson's case. She really was quite lovely.

"Someone was spiteful enough to post a compromising picture of you on StudentSpace.com." Rex felt quite spiteful himself at this point.

"Like that's my body," she scoffed. "The model is at least a double D. And I don't have a tattoo on my ankle."

"I think someone knew about your affair with R.J. and wanted to get back at you without betraying R.J.'s confidence."

R.J. was sharing a room with Justin in his second year. It would be very surprising if Justin didn't know about Ms. Johnson. She was quite a trophy. Most boys wouldn't be able to resist boasting about her.

"Who knew about it?" she demanded.

"I have my suspicions, but that's all they are at this point, and I don't want to add to the rumour mill."

"Al and I have been talking about getting married."

"In my frank opinion, you should lay it all out on the table, Professor. The truth has a way of coming out." He had been caught out over Moira, even though he'd had nothing to hide. Helen had taken a different view of the matter. "If Mr. Cormack finds out, the consequences will be worse. And do you really want to live with the worry of what someone might say or what might appear on the Internet?"

Bethany Johnson looked at her hands. Was that an engagement ring on her finger? "I can run back to my parents' house and get the hoodie," she mumbled.

"It's a bit late now," Rex said, then reconsidered. "Aye, why not?"

"Campbell has a lab this afternoon. I could give it to him."

"Thank you."

"It's not what you think," she said. "I know there are all these cases in the media about female teachers preying on their students, but R.J. was nineteen and very mature for his age."

Rex gave a non-committal nod and left the lab, glad to be out of Bethany Johnson's presence, but probably not as glad as she was to get rid of him.

If R.J. had not murdered Dixon Clark, he wondered feverishly, then who had? Reviewing his list of original suspects, he made straight for Astra Knowles' office.

She was standing by a filing cabinet and sighed when she saw him. "Don' you ever quit, Mr. Graves? Who you looking for now?"

"Klepto."

"Who?"

"Ty Clapham. Know him?"

"I sure do. That kid is one of our brightest stars. His SAT scores were off the chart. He could have gone to an ivy league college, but he got a full scholarship at Hilliard."

"I need his domicile address."

"I'd rather give you his class schedule. Then you could meet him at his lecture hall. He's a psych major." She sat down at her computer and folded her hands on the desk.

"I'd rather see him in his home environment and surprise him."

Ms. Knowles surveyed him over her reading glasses. "Now why would you want to do that?"

"I have something I'd like to return to him in private."

"If you insist." The registrar's multi-ringed fingers flurried across the keyboard. "4312 Arlington Court. It's close to the campus."

Rex retrieved the SUV and, following her directions, entered a respectable neighborhood with freshly mown lawns and shiny cars in the driveways. At #4312 he saw a BMW parked in the garage next to a red Chevy pick-up. The contents of the mailbox confirmed what he already suspected. He rang the bell expectantly. Someone must be home since the garage was wide open.

A yapping bark ripped through the house. When the front door opened, a rat-like creature confronted him from the arms of a lacquered redhead not quite old enough to be Klepto's mother.

"Luella Shaw?"

The woman whipped the cigarette from her lips, releasing a stream of smoke, and peered at him, the sides of her heavily made-up eyes creasing into crow's feet. "Is this about my ex?" she asked suspiciously. A meanness about the mouth hinted that life had not always been a bed of roses and she begrudged every thorn.

"Not as far as I know. Does Ty Clapham live here?"

"Ty-ler!" she screeched, turning toward the interior of the house. Her high-heel mules clicked across the tiled hall, revealing toned legs beneath a short flannel beach wrap.

Klepto appeared in a pair of board shorts, eyes popping out of his head. Rex was pleased to see he had caught the boy at a disadvantage, as planned.

"Don't let all the cold air out the front door," Luella shrilled.

"You'd better come in," Klepto said, glancing up and down the street.

Rex did so.

"Uh, follow me." Klepto led him through the house past a home office containing a treadmill and a master bedroom with an unmade king-size bed. He gestured to a patio table in the lanai where a pair of plastic rafts floated in a kidney-shaped pool.

Rex took a seat, enjoying Klepto's red-faced confusion, each waiting for the other to speak. Gossip magazines covered the glass-top table, along with an overflowing ashtray and numerous pots of glittery nail polish. Removing from his pocket the gray button Klepto had given him the day before at the memorial service, he stuck it in the student's face. "I saw R.J. today," he announced.

"Yeah?"

"He sends his best."

Klepto smirked. "Sure he does."

"I don't know why you thought I'd buy the story about the button. But I think your main objective was to alert me to the fact that your friend Dixon didn't kill himself, and for some reason you didn't want to go to the police with your theory."

"The cops are morons."

"Well, they certainly got the wrong man in the drug bust."

"How do you know for sure that's not R.J.'s button?"

"He no longer has his hoodie. Hasn't had it for months. But I know who does."

Klepto gazed at him, his mouth slightly open, apparently hesitant to say anything and put his foot in it.

"And I don't think he would have rushed out to buy a new one just like it, especially if he intended to visit campus, where security would associate him with the gray-hooded man in the video. If he had intended to go and kill Dixon Clark, I think he would have tried to disguise himself a bit better. So what's the real story behind the button?"

"I found it in Dix's room like I said. I don't know whose it is. It's definitely not Dix's."

"What is your grouse with R.J. Wylie? Is it because he was popular? Had success with the women?"

At that moment Luella slid open the glass door carrying a tray with a jug and two glasses. "I brought y'all some ice tea."

Rex swept aside the magazines to make room. "Most kind. Thank you."

As she bent down to deposit the tray, her wrap fell open revealing a lacy black bra encasing a pair of stretched breasts. Rex pretended not to notice. Her hand, which still held a cigarette, swept to her chest, spilling ash in the jug.

"Okay, Lou. You can go now," Klepto said tightly.

She flounced off, retying her wrap, the hem swirling in the air. She did have a fine pair of legs.

"Not your mother, then?" Rex inquired, knowing perfectly well it wasn't. "She said something about an ex. Did she revert to her maiden name or is Shaw her husband's name?" He poured himself some ice tea, careful not to let any ash tip into his glass. "First or second husband?"

"Second." Klepto spoke in a constrained voice.

Gone were the swagger and insolent repartee of the previous day. Rex knew he was getting to him. "It's an amazing coincidence that StudentSpace.com is registered to Luella." He took a sip of the instant tea that tasted of saccharine and artificial lemon.

"So, you found out I run the site. Congratulations."

"Anyone could have if they'd tried." Rex was not going to implicate his son in the discovery. "The university could not have tried hard enough. Unless, of course, they knew who was behind the site and didn't want to lose one of their scholarship students."

"The dean asked me to tone it down, but these things take on a life of their own."

"It must give you an immense sense of power to control something that has so much influence on people's lives. Why didn't you delete the ditty about your friend?"

"That would be censorship. I do moderate the forums to some extent, but it's a full-time job to read every post and ban people and monitor all that crap."

"That would make your site less popular too, wouldn't it? People crave conflict and confrontation, and your advertisers reward you for the number of hits to your site. Entrepreneurs like you don't give a hoot about the Bill of Rights; you just try to exploit them for all they're worth." Rex found himself becoming as riled as he ever allowed himself to get.

Klepto grabbed the jug and spilt some tea on the table while pouring a glass.

"You're clearly an intelligent young man," Rex said, relenting. "Why not put your talents to better use? Honest work allows you to sleep better at night." Rex hoped he wasn't coming across as too sanctimonious, but he really wanted to get through to the boy. He genuinely deplored seeing a good brain go to waste.

"I sleep fine at night. So, why are you so concerned about my welfare?"

"Because, even though you're not directly responsible for your friend's death, I can't help thinking you're in it for something. I know it was you on the video, not R.J."

"Yeah? Prove it."

"You're the right height for one thing, and when I saw you at the memorial service with your hands in the pockets of that leather jacket, I had a flashback to the video, which I'd just viewed. It was in the body language."

"What are you going to do?"

"What's done is done. We can't put back the clock and spare R.J. all the aggravation he went through on your account, but you can help make things right."

"How?"

"You can tell me who posted that poem about Dixon and his stash."

"It's not that easy to track."

"You can do better than that. I could take that button to the police, tell them you were withholding evidence in a homicide, reveal it was you on video selling coke, even get enough students to file a complaint about how you stole stuff from them. Then I could go to the papers with the story. Local TV vans and reporters would camp in Luella's front yard. How long do you think it would be until she kicked you out? You have it pretty good here. Free use of the BMW, the pool—"

"Okay, look, I think I know who wrote the poem," Klepto cut in. "I listed a chemistry textbook on eBay, but then I noticed that drafts of a poem had been scribbled all over it."

"Do you still have it?"

"Yeah, I couldn't sell it in that state for a decent price. I'll get it for you."

Klepto returned a few minutes later with a hardcover textbook. On the fly leaf was scrawled the name of one Andy Palmer. Inside, written in tiny script in the margin were versions of the Nantucket ditty. Rex imagined him composing it while sitting bored at some lecture.

"Why did Dixon set R.J. up?" he asked.

"I persuaded him that it was R.J. in the video. He genuinely thought it was until it came out in court about the dealer being under six foot. R.J. is a lot taller. Dix figured out it was me, but by then it was too late. R.J. was acquitted anyway, so we thought that would be the end of it."

"Someone wouldn't let it go. They were out for blood." Rex got up, clutching the textbook under his arm. "Thanks for your cooperation. And, Ty? Watch out for those psychopathic tendencies. I hope you learn how to analyze yourself out of them." He paused as he reached the sliding glass doors to the house. "You were bright enough to figure out that Dixon didn't kill himself. Nobody else did."

"What are you going to do now?"

"Whatever it takes."

Resolutely, Rex saw himself out.

TWENTY

When Rex arrived back at the motel, he checked the room phone to see if Helen had called, and was disappointed to see that she had not. He then went for a swim. Performing his fifty laps gave him a chance to review where he was with the case and to rid himself of some of his agitation over the injustice of it all. Klepto and Bethany Johnson were going about their lives as usual, while R.J. was involved in risky construction work with little prospect of ever going back to college. Dixon's murderer had also gone scot-free. Rex was determined to rectify this one perversion of justice.

First he needed to check all the facts so that he would be in a strong position to elicit a confession. This had to be achieved with all speed and efficiency, since tomorrow was his last day to wrap everything up.

Toward 4:00 he headed back to the university and swung by the office of Student Affairs to get the address he needed. As he was leaving, he met Campbell returning from the marine science lab, a plastic bag in his hand.

"This is for you," he told his dad. "Compliments of Ms. Johnson. It's R.J.'s hoodie."

"You peeked?"

"His initials are scrawled on the label. What was she doing with it?"

Ignoring the question, Rex compared the button Klepto had given him to the gray material, just to be sure. It was not a match.

"Want to grab a coffee?" Campbell asked.

"Why not."

"Strange that R.J. is still hanging around Jax," his son remarked. "He could've gone to another college."

"His dad depleted his savings on hiring a lawyer. There's nothing left. He had to take out a second mortgage on his house."

"The college should have paid for R.J. to finish his studies after what they put him through."

"I suppose there was enough proof that he was involved in drugs. And I don't think the dean of students appreciated the wee prank he played on him."

"Sucks for R.J."

A few minutes later, coffee in hand, they gravitated toward the fountain at the center of campus and perched on the stone ledge. The sun filtered through the oak trees, dappling the cropped grass with light. A soft breeze wafted across the open space. Students in T-shirts and tank tops milled about, in no apparent hurry to be indoors on such a mellow afternoon.

"So what's new?" Campbell asked. "Are you going to solve the case by the time we leave Saturday?"

"With any luck, but I'd prefer not to tell you about it just yet. You might inadvertently give something away, and I don't want the culprit catching on."

"It's not someone I know, is it?"

"It's someone conspicuous by their absence at the memorial service. And that's all I'm telling you."

Campbell sighed, knowing better than to persist in his questions.

"I can tell you that Klepto is the mastermind behind Student-Space.com," Rex told him.

"I know. It's gone viral. He posted a blog saying he was being suspended as of today until he shut it down. He's asking students to vote for or against the college's decision. There's talk of a riot. The consensus is that Hilliard is in violation of the First Amendment by forcing him to abort it."

"Free speech among students is typically protected in this country, except where it disrupts educational activities or invades the rights of others."

"Someone leaked that the Clarks were going to sue the school," Campbell said around a mouthful of bagel. "They're claiming the libel on SS.com pushed Dix over the edge and Hilliard did nothing to prevent it. I suppose the Clarks would have to go after the school since Klepto hasn't got any money."

"I don't know if the Clarks are aware yet of who runs Student-Space.com. And, anyway, I don't think it's the money they're after; it's the principle. They feel the university should protect the welfare of its students first and foremost. I found out from Student Affairs that Klepto was the webmaster for the school's official site in his first year. I went to see him at his home. That's where he runs his operation."

"Did you see his fancy lady?"

"Luella Shaw."

"She's the one the website is registered to! What's she like?"

"A wee bit trashy, to be honest. I suppose she must have done quite well out of her divorce settlement. Four-bedroom house, double garage, pool."

At that moment, Campbell's gaze drifted to a couple walking hand in hand on the far side of campus. "Isn't that Mike and Kris? I wonder how long they've been dating."

"They were sitting together at the memorial service."

"I didn't notice."

"Well, you only had eyes for Melodie." He turned toward Campbell, determined to broach an important matter. Something had been bothering Rex since he had seen Mike at the Student Health Center. He decided to try the direct approach. "Son, I wanted to talk to you about STDs."

Campbell stared at him in abject horror.

"I picked up a leaflet at the Health Center on campus," Rex explained.

"What were you doing there?"

"I went to see the medical professional who prescribed Xanax to Dixon."

"Dad, I don't have any STDs. I don't have indiscriminate sex and I don't do drugs, for your information. I know you've been dying to ask me."

"None at all?"

"Occasionally I hit the bong, that's all. I get a natural high from surfing and playing guitar."

Rex slumped with relief on the fountain ledge. "Thank you for putting my mind at ease."

"You smoke a pipe. I never even touch cigarettes."

"Point taken." Campbell was very good on the offensive, which was, come to think of it, his position in soccer.

"You didn't really think I was on drugs, did you?"

"Truth to tell, I didn't know what to think. I was that worried."

"Was it Grandma who put the idea in your head? She worries about everything."

"Don't I know it? No, I didn't tell her about our phone conversation. She thinks I came out here on a whim."

"I was feeling stressed. It's been strained around here since R.J. was arrested." Campbell regarded him with curiosity. "Didn't you ever experiment with drugs?"

"Pot is five times stronger now than it was in my day."

"Where did you read that?"

"At the university library."

"You've been spending a lot of time there."

"Aye. Funny how I never saw you there once." Punching his son jovially on the shoulder, Rex got up off the fountain ledge. "See you later. I need to go find someone."

He calculated that by 5:00 most classes would be out and Andy Palmer would be back in his dorm, but after knocking fruitlessly at the door for fifteen minutes, he gave up and went to try Campus Security. After much persuasion, the guard looked up Palmer's parking permit registration and told Rex which lot he had been assigned and what vehicle he drove.

Rex looked around Parking C for a yellow Hyundai Elantra. No car fit that description. There was nothing to do but bide his time until Palmer returned. Rex desperately hoped the author of the Nantucket poem had not taken off for an early weekend. In the meantime, there was one other thing he could do.

He had found out from Campus Security the number of the detective at the Jacksonville Police Department who had arrested R.J. Wylie. Rex formed an instant dislike upon first phone contact. Beecham didn't want to be reminded of his error, but as soon as Rex mentioned he might have a homicide case all wrapped up and ready for the detective to close, he became more attentive. Not only a homicide, Rex told him; he would provide the real culprit in the drug bust, and Beecham could explain away the confusion between two similarly dressed boys of the same age. Rex felt he was bargaining with the devil, yet he needed proof of Klepto's involvement to completely exonerate R.J.

"Talk to my informant," the detective grunted into the phone. "Guy by the name of Wayne Price. You'll find him at The Shamrock this evening."

At the appointed time, Rex found himself in a murky sports bar with big screen TVs at each corner and a green patterned carpet reeking of beer. Most of the customers were loners. He had taken the precaution of tucking a slim voice recorder in his breast pocket.

Before he was halfway to the bar, he recognized the police informant from the video. At first glance, Wayne Price could pass for thirty, but as Rex approached he saw he was closer to forty. A wariness in the eyes and a hard set about the shoulders hinted at time served in prison. As a prosecutor, Rex could tell a seasoned felon a mile off. He slid onto the stool beside Price and ordered a beer, attempting to look casual and not as though he had wandered onto a bad American cop show.

"You the guy wanted to see me 'bout the student bust?" Price asked, swinging around and surveying the room. "Make it snappy. If I pull out my cell phone, it means you gotta leave."

The detective had told him Price was working on a bust that night. He'd make sure Price was cooperative but warned Rex not to blow his cover.

"I saw Clark's video. It's on the Internet," Rex said, wasting no time. He set the photo of the Phi Beta Kappa fraternity, procured online, on the bar top under a newspaper, which he used to nudge the photo in Price's direction. "Who was really selling to you?"

The informant picked up his drink. "Top far right," he muttered, glancing first at the picture and then away again. "The one in the green polo shirt."

"You're sure?"

"Yeah, I'd recognize that cocky asshole anywhere."

"So why did you testify it was R.J. Wylie?"

"Beecham told me that's who I bought from. I'm on a suspended sentence courtesy of the JPD. My privileges can be revoked anytime they don't like what I say. Beecham said to make it stick."

"Did Wylie ever confess?"

"No, but he never did produce his hoodie neither. The police wanted to test it for coke residue to get a match with the blow I bought off him. The hoodie mysteriously vanished. The cops thought that made him guilty as hell."

"His girlfriend had it. He was protecting her."

"Looks like he got shafted both ways, don't it?"

"Why would there be residue on the jacket?"

"The bag I got was split. The dealer had it in his pocket."

"It doesn't bother you that the wrong lad got busted?"

"This cokehead or that one … What difference does it make?"

"One life. Almost two. Wylie didn't sell."

"So he's up for sainthood?"

Rex thought he should leave before he threw the informant across the bar and made him wish he'd gone back to prison. "Thanks for identifying the dealer," he said tonelessly, preparing to depart.

"It's the one I pointed out in the photo. For real. Wylie, the student I fingered for the police, was taller, a nice, easy-going kid. He never let the cops push him into a confession. I think that got up Beecham's nose."

"Why do you think the police set so much store by what Dixon Clark said?"

"White middle-class boy, doin' his job monitoring illegal drug activity in the dorms. Beecham wanted a collar." Price glanced around before murmuring into his glass. "Heard something from my cop pals about the Clark suicide. It'll cost you a twenty."

"Is it worth twenty?"

"Pay up and see."

Rex surreptitiously pushed a bill under the newspaper.

"The Clark kid was loaded with Xanax. The overdose details weren't released to the press. The school didn't want reporters shining a spotlight on prescription drug abuse among its students." Price pulled a cell phone from the pocket of his cheap denim shirt. "Sure been nice talking to you," he told Rex.

Taking his cue, Rex got up from his stool, retrieved the photograph from off the bar, and walked toward the pub entrance, eager to see if the Elantra was in the campus parking lot. He could not wait to put a lid on this case so he could discharge his promise to the Clarks and take off for the Keys without a care in the world—other than whether Helen would talk to him ever again.

TWENTY–ONE

DISAPPOINTED TO FIND THAT Andy Palmer had not returned to campus, Rex wandered back to the dorms. As he entered Keynes Hall, he heard a muted drum cadence topped by a clash of cymbals. He followed the sound to the basement where Campbell and two other band members, including Red, were setting up their instruments.

A black youth with a shaved head and the lithe grace of a panther grabbed an acoustic guitar from its stand and strapped it over his shoulder.

"Dad, meet Dominic."

"I'm the one with the sex appeal." Dominic reached over his guitar and clasped Rex's hand with a smile that lit up the basement with the dazzling whiteness of halogen bulbs.

Rex leaned against a rickety ping pong table, waiting for the band to start. The sagging couches along the walls were already taken, in some cases double occupancy as girls squeezed onto boys' laps. Other students perched on the industrial-size washers and dryers. A few had brought chairs and mini kegs. The atmosphere grew festive as the electric and base guitarists adjusted their amps and debated the play list.

As the trio launched into a rap version of "Every 1's a Winner" by Hot Chocolate, the audience responded with ear-splitting whistles and enthusiast applause. Students continued to trickle into the basement, lounging between the ping pong table and the band on its makeshift platform. The backsides of coeds in low-cut jeans swung like pendulums in time to the music. Some of the girls had impressive assets. Rex preferred a big bottom to a skinny one any day of the week and enjoyed the view immensely.

The music was endorphic, pulsing through his veins and striking a chord in his very soul. The audience clapped along in perfect tempo and cheered at the end of the song, including Rex. A boy thrust a plastic mug of beer into his hand and Rex raised it in a toast. The funky aroma of weed blended with body heat, and he began to develop a buzz from the combination of alcoholic and hallucinogenic influences.

He didn't recognize the next piece, but it had a good beat, with an undertone of reggae, and the musicians played in sync. Red, in a black T-shirt with sleeves shorn at the shoulders, showed off muscles glistening with sweat as he pounded on his drum set. Campbell played a fair accompaniment, but Dom was the star. His voice flowed rich, smooth, and suggestive. Campbell backed him up on vocals. Rex hadn't known he could sing. He certainly hadn't inherited that particular talent from his dad.

Rex finished his beer, made sure his camera was on flash, and took a picture. The music and audience had grown so loud that it took a few seconds for the crowd to react when an explosion shook the wall and rattled the panes in the windows. Voices and instruments trailed to a ragged halt as everyone turned toward the noise.

"What *was* that?"

"Thunder, I guess."

"An earthquake?"

"This ain' California, bro."

"Power's still on."

Students gathered at the windows while others made for the door.

"See those fires over by the admin buildings?" an observer at the window declared. "What's up with that?"

The band remained in position, hampered by their instruments and waiting to see if they should resume playing. Rex's gaze crossed Campbell's.

"I'll go check it out."

"I'm coming with you." Campbell zipped up his guitar in its carrying case and scrambled after his dad.

Outside, twilight was falling. An eerie silence reigned, punctured by shouts on the far side of the campus. Police sirens wailed in the distance. As Rex and Campbell crossed the berm dividing the residence halls from the faculty buildings, flames shot out in front of the administrative tower up ahead. Campbell stowed his guitar in the SUV while Rex went to investigate.

Dashing through Parking C, he spotted a yellow Hyundai Elantra. A human shadow flitted into the oak trees. Rex ran on. The chants of protest intensified as he skirted the building that housed the main offices. Torched vehicles blazed in the front parking lot, spewing plumes of black smoke. Someone had spray-painted "HO" in white letters across Al Cormack's green Saturn. Rex knew enough American slang to realize that they weren't simply misspelling a gardening implement. Nor did it require a stretch of the imagination to figure out that the slut referred to must be the math professor's girlfriend, Bethany Johnson.

A crowd of two hundred students waved placards defending the right to free speech on cyberspace. Others condemned StudentSpace.com for causing Dixon Clark's death. One sign depicted a noose. Rex recognized a brushed leather jacket among the throng.

"Might have known," he said in Klepto's ear.

The psych major spun around to face him. "Did you hear about my suspension? Whatever happened to freedom of expression?"

"I suppose it got abused. Who set fire to the cars?"

Klepto hoisted his shoulders. "Beats me. The Molotovs were lobbed from those trees over there. A faculty meeting is taking place inside the auditorium to decide how to handle the Clarks' lawsuit. The dean of students came out before all hell broke loose and threatened to call the cops if we didn't disperse. Then the vice president's car got hit, as did a couple of others."

"Did you incite this riot?"

"I never suggested we resort to violence. I just wanted to save my website. It was supposed to be a peaceful demonstration."

"Well, someone stole your thunder."

At that moment a bottle whizzed over their heads and smashed through a second-story window. Flames leaped up from the darkness within the office. Suddenly, illuminated by a burning car, two dark figures exchanged punches. An all-out fight erupted, rippling to the farthest reaches of the crowd. A few students dropped their signs and ran. More followed as police and fire truck sirens drew near. The diehard protesters merged, falling upon each other with bloodcurdling screams. Rex raced back toward the SUV, yanking Campbell along with him.

"If we don't get out of here now, we'll get stuck in a police road block," he said, panting.

"There's a mud track along the river bank. It's bumpy, but it'll take us to the main road two miles farther down."

"Let's go."

The yellow Elantra was gone from the student parking lot, leaving tell-tale white paint drips in its vacated space.

"He beat us to it."

"Who did?" Campbell asked.

"The graffiti artist."

Rex let Campbell drive, since he knew the way. The headlights set at low beam barely emitted enough light to guide them over the rough terrain.

"You weren't joking about the bumpy ride," Rex remarked, jolted about in the passenger seat.

"You couldn't do this in your Mini Cooper," Campbell pointed out smugly.

"It's not every day I try to evade the police."

Twenty minutes later they were headed downtown. Campbell took a turn onto Interstate 95.

"Back to the Siesta?" he asked.

"Aye, but let's stop by the Publix deli on the way. We can picnic on the bed and watch a movie."

"I told you something was up on SS.com. I should call Red, find out what's new." Campbell reached into his jeans pocket.

"You're not phoning and driving at the same time."

"Da-ad!"

"Wait 'til we stop. By the way, sorry your gig got interrupted. It seemed to be a huge success."

"But don't give up my degree?" Campbell inquired with a devilish grin.

"Get your degree, and then you're on your own. I'll wish you the best in whatever you decide to do, as long as it's legal and nothing that would make your grandmother blush."

"How does she feel about male strippers?"

"She probably thinks they renovate furniture."

"I won't tell her if you don't," Campbell joked.

By the time they reached the motel room, loaded with groceries, news of the university riot had hit the local news station. A female reporter was talking excitedly into a mike with the administrative building behind her and a posse of police cars flashing red and blue lights in the foreground. The fires had been extinguished, and wreaths of smoke spiraled skyward from the parking lot.

"A frenzied mob of students torched the vice president's car and went on a rampage, destroying college property," she announced. "Police quelled the uprising with tear gas. A dozen undergraduates have been taken into custody. The riot ostensibly arose out of a threat by the university to shut down a student website, but at the heart of the matter appears to be a controversy involving the expulsion of a sophomore earlier this year.

"Another student whose memorial service was held at St. Peter's Episcopal Church yesterday afternoon is said to have been instrumental in the expulsion. Dixon Clark's death in his dorm room at the weekend was ruled a suicide. The website, StudentSpace.com, incited the passions of supporters of both undergraduates, culminating in a clash of violence this evening."

The next clip showed the dean of students in his academic gown standing by the entrance. "Of course we at Hilliard believe in the First Amendment," he said grimly, "but there comes a point where we must consider the well-being of our students. This is not about freedom of speech but violation of university policy, as this recent demonstration has shown. We are carefully looking into the matter and will take appropriate action."

"Where's the president of Hilliard in all this?" Rex asked as he brought the wrapped subs to the bed.

"He's on a fund-raising tour of alumni. Justin saw a janitor carry Dix's PC out of his dorm late yesterday afternoon."

"They won't have found anything if you wiped it clean, but the Clarks might have informed the college they were now in receipt of emails their son sent to the faculty. That might explain why Hilliard finally took steps to shut down the website. Did Red say who was arrested when you spoke on the phone?"

"Klepto, for one. Nobody I know personally."

"Then they haven't got the ringleader."

Rex wondered if news of the riot would reach the Clarks. He could not help but think the university had mishandled the whole situation from start to finish. But then, Dr. Binkley hadn't reckoned on an evil, elusive force being at work all that time, a force still at large.

TWENTY–TWO

By the time Rex and Campbell returned to Hilliard early the next morning, police had cordoned off the administrative area with yellow crime tape. Charred skeletons of cars bore witness to the previous night's violence. The window on the second floor was boarded up and mimicked a closed eye. Students huddled in groups about the perimeter gawking at the scene.

"What a mess," Rex said as he drove to the residential blocks on the west side of campus.

He was relieved to see the yellow Elantra parked in its spot. He followed his son into Keynes Hall and, turning off on the second floor, continued to the far end of the corridor where he had waited the day before. He prayed he would have better luck this time.

Unable to detect any sound through the door, he knocked discreetly. At this point he heard scuffling and the opening and shutting of drawers. He knocked louder and again encountered silence.

"I know you're in there, Andy," he called. "It's Campbell's dad. Open up."

The door opened a fraction, and a mousy-haired boy with glasses askew on his nose appeared in the gap, dressed in a wrinkled white T-shirt half hanging out of his jeans.

"Let me in, lad. This is not the sort of conversation you want everyone in the corridor to hear."

Palmer shut the door behind them. Clothes, textbooks, CDs, fast food containers, and loose sheets of paper were scattered across the linoleum floor and piled up on the shelf beneath the window and over part of the bed. Rex leaned against the wooden closet, arms folded, while Palmer sank on the navy blue comforter, hands hanging between his bony knees.

"I didn't catch your name when you were in Campbell's room Monday morning with Red, Mike, and Justin. It is Andy, isn't it?"

The boy shrugged his narrow shoulders. "Or Four-Eyes."

"Where did you pick up that nickname?"

"Middle school. I'll get contacts as soon as I can afford them."

Rex thought there was nothing wrong with glasses, although Palmer's heavy frames made him look like Woody Allen. "Andy, I have proof you wrote the infamous Nantucket poem."

"What proof?"

"Your name is inside the chemistry book Klepto stole, which has revisions of the poem all over it. *'There once was a man from Nantucket who kept all his stash in a bucket.'* So, Dix wouldn't share his stash?"

"I wasn't in his clique. He sold two milligrams of Xanax for four bucks a bar. He'd been stockpiling it since high school. D'you know how much those mothers cost online without a prescription? Dix was a hypocrite and a snitch. I just wanted to party. I mixed them with alcohol. And then I got hooked."

"Drugs will impair brain function, lad. Is that what made you do it?"

"Do what?"

"Let's start with that nude picture of Ms. Johnson. Did you post it?"

"Why would I do that?"

"To embarrass her. You couldn't come right out and tell people she was having an affair with R.J. because he swore you to secrecy. So you got back at her anonymously for not coming to your friend's defense."

"Wha-what do you want?" The boy's fingers clawed at his hands. Rex noticed he had a bad case of eczema.

"Have you got something for that rash?" he asked.

Palmer looked at his hands. "I've had it since I was a kid."

"You must have had a tough time in school. It's not easy being picked on. R.J. protected you from the bullies. So you decided to come to Hilliard with him. I met R.J. His heart is in the right place."

"He always had my back. I got respect because he was my friend."

Rex nodded, remembering his school days. "I knew someone like that: Kevin McVie. Captain of just about every sport. All the girls fancied him because he had the looks and the charm."

"What happened to him?"

"He became a member of Parliament. He's on his third expensive divorce now, according to the tabloid news."

"Women will get you every time."

"That's a right cynical attitude, young man. Do you speak from experience?"

Palmer shrugged weakly.

"You have a girlfriend?"

"There was someone, or so I thought. She confided in me about her problems with Dix over coffee one time. But it didn't work out."

"She's dating someone else?"

"Yeah. It happened so fast. You met him—Mike."

"Oh, aye. The Colts fan from Indiana."

"That's him."

"That's not why you killed Dixon, though, is it? Because of Kris?"

Rex watched as Palmer's mouth worked with emotion but no words came out. "I found this in Dixon's room." He showed the boy the button.

Before Palmer could say anything, Rex opened the closet and began scanning the messy shelves. He almost missed the gray hoodie hanging between the other clothes. He pulled it off the hanger. A frayed thread hung from the neck where a button was missing. "Look, what do you know... It's a perfect match."

"Someone must've planted it."

"The same someone who left the suicide instructions on the desk? That doesn't make sense. The murderer wanted to make Dixon's death look like suicide. He wouldn't have left a button belonging to someone else there. Why did you do it?"

"I didn't."

Rex lifted a tangle of damp towels off a stray chair and dragged it close to the bed. That way the boy couldn't bolt from the room. He spread the hoodie on his lap. "A garment like this would come

179

in handy for sliding through vents and carrying a rope and a set of suicide instructions in these wide pockets..."

"That's crazy!"

"Not really. You and R.J. were study-buddies. Isn't that the term you employ in the States? You were both majoring in chemistry. You must have been in his room many times."

"Lots of people hung out in his room. Where did you find the button?"

"By Dixon's chair, after he was found swinging from the rope. How did your button get there? You weren't a friend of Dixon's and you weren't around when I broke down his door. You didn't attend his memorial service either. You are a very elusive character, Andy. After I met you, you vanished from my radar. Then last night you throw fire bombs to get back at the university for expelling R.J. and you vandalize Cormack's car to punish Bethany Johnson some more for not sticking up for your friend. Is the spray can still in your car or did you dispose of it?"

"I didn't do any of those things."

"You did it all for R.J.," Rex ploughed on inexorably. If he could get a confession out of Palmer, he could write up his report and email it to Mr. Clark. Then he could turn his attention to the more pleasant prospect of his trip to the Keys. "You saw a way to repay R.J. for his kindness to you. You didn't mean to kill Dixon, but things got out of hand."

"I have no idea what you're talking about."

"You wanted R.J. back on campus. He stuck up for you against the bullies at Dunbar High in Fort Myers."

"How do you know about Dunbar?"

"I spoke to R.J.'s dad. He said R.J. was still in touch with an old friend from high school. Later on, I remembered the Miami Dolphins shirt from the morning I met you, so I guessed you were from Florida."

"Dunbar is a rough school. Lots of black kids, just like here."

"You worked with R.J. in his dad's pool business."

"Yeah. Why d'you wanna know?"

"Chlorine tablets cause explosions if mixed with the right stuff. You'd know that from treating swimming pools. You manufactured those Molotov cocktails. A piece of cake for a chemistry major. *You* sparked the riot."

"Lots of students saw the injustice of R.J.'s expulsion and joined in on StudentSpace.com."

"Doesn't do to get on the wrong side of you, does it, Andy? Sounds to me like you can take care of yourself without R.J. Downloading the instructions was a clever move. It's difficult composing a convincing suicide note. Harder than writing a ditty."

Andy hung his head.

"Turn yourself in, lad. It'll go easier for you and give Dixon's parents some closure. They're eating themselves up wondering why their son killed himself."

"He wasn't supposed to wind up dead. I thought if he signed a confession saying he had falsely accused R.J. of selling blow, R.J. had a chance of getting back into Hilliard. But Dix wouldn't sign it, even when I threatened to punch his lights out. He didn't want to face disciplinary action."

Rex almost laughed at the idea of this skinny geek punching the lights out of anyone. "What did you threaten him with to get him up on that chair?"

"Nothing. He was acting all weird. Said he had a stomach bug or the flu, or something. Anyway, he was kinda dizzy and disoriented."

"He had a lot of Xanax in his system. That must have made it easier to force him onto the chair and put a noose around his neck."

"It wasn't that easy. I had to turn the music way up on his boom box and gag him. I told him I was going to leave him standing on the chair with the rope around his neck and his hands tied until he agreed to sign the confession."

"What did you use to bind his wrists?"

"A silk tie."

That was why no marks had been found on Dixon's wrists. "Where is the tie now?"

"I burnt it. I put the instructions on how to commit suicide on his desk to show I was serious. I said I'd pull the chair out from under him. A confession was the only way to clear R.J., but Dix struggled and accidentally kicked over the chair himself. I heard Kris at the door and panicked."

"Then you made your way back up through the ceiling to R.J.'s old room while my son was out in the corridor."

"Justin said Campbell would be gone all weekend. He asked me to fill in for him on the soccer team. I borrowed the spare key Campbell gave him." As Palmer's head dropped in his hands, his glasses fell to the floor. He looked up blindly. "It's not what you think. I just wanted to get Dix to sign a confession so R.J. could get back on campus."

"The bullied doing the bullying."

"Just because Dix was an RA, he thought that made him something special. I don't know what Kris saw in him. He wasn't even faithful to her. She said she had caught something nasty off him." The boy retrieved his glasses from the floor and hooked them back on behind his large ears. "What'll I get? Could I just get sentenced to rehab?"

"I don't know what the sentencing guidelines are here."

Back home, the youths he prosecuted often came from broken homes and had little education. Drug addiction was rarely a get-out-of-jail free card for them. "If you explain everything to the police the way you did to me, you could receive a lighter sentence. I might be able to persuade Dixon's parents to be merciful."

Palmer wrung his hands. "I went over and over the plan in my head, but I never meant to kill him when it came down to it. It was an accident."

"How about we go talk to the police?" Rex handed him his hoodie. "Take this," he said. "It can get cold in jail."

After entrusting Palmer into the care of Detective Beecham at the police station with a summary of what he had found out pertaining to Dixon Clark's death and the real identity of the student on the drug bust video, Rex decided a visit to the dean of students was in order. A uniformed cop was standing guard at the entrance to the college administrative building and asked him his business.

"I'm a parent, here to see Dr. Binkley."

At the mention of his name, the dean, standing in the lobby, turned around and held out his hand. "Mr. Graves. How are you? We had some trouble on campus last night as I'm sure you're aware."

"I've come to see you on a related matter."

Rex pulled the voice recorder from his shirt pocket and re-played the conversation with Wayne Price at The Shamrock. "The police informant on the tape positively identified Ty Clapham of his own volition," he informed the dean. "R.J. Wylie never con-fessed to the detective who arrested him. He couldn't produce the hoodie because it was in Professor Johnson's possession and she would not come forward in his defense."

"Bethany Johnson, our assistant marine science professor? Do I infer that she and R.J. Wylie…"

"Infer what you like, Dean. She provided me with the hoodie in question when I confronted her about it."

"I see."

"The case against Wylie was a flimsy fabrication and it was thrown out with good reason. Fortunately the jury showed better judgment than the faculty at Hilliard."

The dean of students cleared his throat. "I'll, ah, review Wylie's case. Well, thank you for all you have done." He vigorously shook Rex's hand. "Have a safe trip home."

"Now that you have clear proof it wasn't R.J. on the video, wouldn't the right thing to do be to reinstate him?"

Rex didn't wait for an answer before walking off through the main doors in the direction of Keynes Hall. He had one final task to accomplish, the hardest so far.

TWENTY—THREE

LATER THAT MORNING, AFTER he had heard back from the dean and while his son was at a lecture, Rex sat down at Campbell's laptop to write to the Clarks, assisted by the American spell-checker.

Dear Mr. & Mrs. Clark:

Much as this news will undoubtedly come as a fresh shock, I must inform you that it appears Dixon did not in fact commit suicide, but was murdered by a student named Andy Palmer. The motive he gave me was that he had known R.J. Wylie—the boy who was erroneously implicated by Dixon in a drug deal—since high school, and was seeking to right the wrong of his friend's expulsion from Hilliard University.

Andy Palmer studied with R.J. Wylie, also a chemistry major, in his room and discovered access to Dixon's room below through the air ducts. Being under the effects of a sedative, Dixon was less able to put up a defense than he might otherwise have been. Andy forced him onto a chair (possibly with the aid of a weapon)

*and put a rope around his neck. He showed him the suicide in-
structions he had brought with him. The plan was to coerce
Dixon into signing a written confession to falsely accusing R.J.
Wylie. According to Andy, Dixon knocked over the chair while
struggling to get free. Andy panicked and fled the scene.*

*The dealer in the phone video was Dixon's ex-roommate,
Tyler Clapham ("Klepto"), who managed to convince Dixon to
incriminate R.J. Wylie instead. Klepto, while not a direct culprit
in Dixon's death, acted as a catalyst for the tragic sequence of
events. He is the webmaster of StudentSpace.com, which the
university is now attempting to shut down. Klepto has been suspended pending a full inquiry into his role in the drug deal that
resulted in R.J.'s expulsion and ultimately in your son's death.*

*In conclusion, R.J. Wylie, an able student, was falsely ac-
cused of drug-dealing and has, as far as I can ascertain, never
sold drugs. His high school friend Andy Palmer wished to re-
dress this wrong, and events spiraled out of control. Dixon, it
seems, also refused to sell Andy the Xanax at the price he was
selling it to his friends, and this angered Andy, who is responsible for posting the Nantucket poem.*

*I should add that R.J. is not a completely innocent party in
all this, since he was using cocaine, contrary to dorm rules, at
the time of his arrest. He is now clean and mentoring kids in
an anti-drugs program.*

*These are the facts as I understand them. I will follow up
by phone at the weekend.*

Yours sincerely,
Rex Graves, Q.C.

He hoped a couple of days would be enough time for Dixon's parents to absorb the impact of the email before he spoke with them. As it turned out, Keith Clark called him within the hour.

"It's been an emotional roller-coaster," he admitted. "Katherine and I have been talking about the situation since we got your email. First of all, we are so very grateful for your involvement; otherwise we would never have gotten at the truth of what happened."

He took a deep breath. "We spoke to the dean by phone a short while ago, and he confirmed that the website has been shut down. He is amenable to re-enrolling R.J. Wylie, subject to regular drug screening, and provided that the school's action is not construed as an admission of culpability. R.J. may have to make up some classes in the summer. We agreed not to pursue a lawsuit against Hilliard, and we've decided to help R.J. with his tuition fees."

"That is truly generous of you and Katherine," Rex said in admiration. "Does R.J. know about this yet?"

"I spoke to his father. The poor man broke down. The stress he's been under must have been intolerable. He took out a second mortgage on his house to pay for his son's defense. I understand that R.J. is currently working construction to pay off the loan."

"Aye, he's working at the top of a skyscraper."

"Well, I wouldn't want my son doing that. In any case, Katherine and I had been thinking about setting up a scholarship in Dixon's name. Under the circumstances, we think R.J. should benefit instead."

Rex gave a heartfelt sigh. "I believe it's a good decision. I've had the opportunity to talk to R.J. at length. He's a bright lad and should have had a bright future. Thanks to you, he'll still have that chance. I don't think he'll make the same mistake twice."

"We don't always get second chances for ourselves or our kids. The next best thing is to be able to provide them."

"I'll call you in a few days and let you know how we're getting on at the cottage."

"Please do. Have a great time down there."

As Rex closed his phone, a mingling of sadness and optimism overcame him. Mr. Clark's words moved him to tears. Just when you thought all hope was lost for humanity, along came someone who restored your faith in mankind. What a great moment it would be for R.J. when he got the news.

TWENTY—FOUR

"So, how does it feel to solve a case?" Kris asked Rex. She was seated beside Mike at the trestle table in the student quad.

A group of Campbell's friends had barbecued hamburgers and hot dogs for a late lunch.

"Och, it's the best feeling in the world."

"I heard Four-Eyes is copping to Man Two," Justin said, squirting mustard onto a bread roll.

"The police searched his car and found a switchblade," Dominic countered. "Won't that make a difference?"

"Not if the plea already went down," Justin said.

"Yeah, well he probably threatened Dixon with the knife. How else would he have gotten him up on a chair? Dumb that he left the weapon in his car."

"That's where he keeps it, I guess. Jax is a dangerous place, bro'. I got protection myself."

Rex listened to the debate between Justin and Dominic, glad that he was not the one to have to mete out punishment.

"I just can't see it. I mean, Four-Eyes?" Mike shook his head in disbelief. "Involuntary manslaughter. Whoa. And then he went ballistic, throwing incendiary bombs all over campus. I wonder if Klepto will be expelled."

"The video is fuzzy," Rex told Mike. "Unless the police can enhance it in some way, it will be hard to prove who was selling to the informant, in spite of his new testimony."

"Klepto will wriggle out of any charges," Justin put in. "He's manipulative and controlling. He managed to convince Dix that the dealer in the video was R.J."

"Klepto was jealous of R.J." Rex added, "I'm not sure R.J. knows the good news yet."

"You deserve to deliver it to him. You made it all happen. You are way cool, Mr. Graves."

"Why, thank you, Kris. I think I will, unless someone has beaten me to the punch. And thanks for the sendoff party." Rex dabbed at his mouth with a paper napkin. "I'll see you back here," he told Campbell. "Make sure you're all packed and ready to go. We'll be leaving the Siesta Inn first thing in the morning."

He phoned Tony at the construction site and told him he was headed over there right now.

"R.J. knocks off at three-thirty," the project manager informed him. "His dad called me with the news. Looks like I'm going to lose a good worker."

"Does R.J. know yet?"

"Nah. I thought I'd wait until the end of his shift. Don't want him falling off the building in his excitement. It's a long way down, as you know." Tony guffawed.

"Aye, make sure he stays safe until I get there. I'd like to tell him myself."

"Be my guest. He'd never believe it from me anyhow. He'd think I was pulling his leg."

With a warm feeling of anticipation, Rex closed his phone and climbed into the SUV. He made good time in spite of Friday afternoon traffic. As he arrived, the crew was descending the gleaming bronze tower in the outdoor elevators. R.J. was among the first to reach the gate, paycheck in hand.

"Hey," he said when he saw Rex. "What brings you back here?"

"Ms. Johnson returned this."

R.J. stared at the hoodie for a long time as he turned it around in hands that were dry and cracked with gray concrete dust. "What did she say?"

"That she was sorry."

R.J. nodded. His throat made a low choking sound.

"For what it's worth, I know for a fact you had nothing to do with Dixon's death."

"Do you know who did it?"

"Aye. I guess no one has told you yet. You won't be happy."

"My dad?"

"Why would you think that?"

"He came to visit last weekend. He was real mad at Dix Clark."

"No, it wasna your dad. Have you spoken with him yet?"

"Why?"

"First I better tell you about your friend Andy Palmer."

R.J. stared at him with a mixture of curiosity and dread. "What about him?"

"It was Andy who murdered Dixon Clark."

"Four-Eyes? No way, man!"

"Are you still in touch with him?"

"He calls from time to time to let me know what's new on campus."

"Did he tell you about Mr. Cormack and Bethany?"

"Yeah, and about Clark's suicide, right after it happened. He sounded a bit hyper. Now I know why."

"The Clarks set up a college fund in their son's name and want to give it to you."

"Are you kidding me?"

Rex smiled all the way to his ears and shook his head. "They realize Dixon was misguidedly instrumental in your arrest and they want to make amends, provided you continue to keep off the drugs. The dean of students is agreeable to your resuming your studies."

"Binkley actually said that?"

"Yes, we had a long conversation on the phone."

"If I go back to Hilliard, I'll talk to freshmen about how drugs can trash your life," R.J. promised. "Oh, wow, I can really go back?"

"Monday."

R.J. pulled off his hard hat and hurled it with exuberance into the air. "But why did Andy do it?" he asked, catching the hat adroitly in his left hand.

"He felt he owed it to you for always protecting him."

"Dumbass. Is he in jail?"

Rex told R.J. where the boy was being held until his arraignment. "He's also facing charges of destruction of university property."

"I saw about the riot on the news. His family doesn't have any money. They live in a trailer. Shit." R.J. stared morosely at the ground before perking up again. "I'll go visit him right now."

Rex held out his hand. "I wish you all the best at Hilliard."

R.J. grabbed it. "Thanks for everything. Are you headed back home?"

"I'm going to the Keys with Campbell first. But I'll be back at some point."

"Be sure to look me up."

"Will do."

Rex walked away with a sense of satisfaction. R.J. was a good lad at heart and deserved his second chance. Rex only hoped he himself would get a second chance with Helen.

TWENTY—FIVE

THE COAST ROAD ALONG Ponte Verde Beach was clear of traffic at this hour of the morning. Rex drove with one eye on the Atlantic Ocean, already glimmering with the first rays of sun beyond the swaying stalks of sea oats, the view intermittently interrupted by stilt homes backing onto the sand.

His mind dwelled on Helen. He was still kicking himself for telling her that Moira's visit wasn't important. That was always a mistake to say to women, who apparently thought everything was important, however trivial-seeming to men. They had not spoken since he had called her from the waiting room at the hospital when Moira was first admitted. She had not returned his messages. In spite of his determination not to let it spoil his trip, he could not help but feel a cold dread in his heart that Helen had dumped him.

"Did you get an exemption from your Monday class?" he asked Campbell, to get his mind off her.

"You already asked me that. I'm clear through Tuesday."

Campbell's phone *dringed*. He read the text message and beamed.

"From Melodie?" Rex asked hopefully.

"How did you know?"

"Because when you get a message from Consuela, you usually scowl."

"Melly has invited me to stay in Nantucket over the summer vacation. She says she took Dix's Easter bunny back to college with her, and that it's a relief to look at it and know her brother didn't take his own life."

"Did she knit that bunny?"

"Aye."

Rex would bet his bottom dollar that Consuela did not knit. "Will you still be seeing Miss Cuba in Miami?"

"I may stop by and tell her I want to take time out of the relationship." Campbell sighed blissfully at his cell phone. "I should add being in love to my list of natural highs. I never knew what it felt like before."

"And you were just saying how grand it would be to take a break from women and go fishing," Rex teased. "Will you be okay driving back all this way by yourself?"

"I've made the trip before."

"I know, Son ... Sometimes I don't give you enough credit."

"You're going to love the wildlife in the Keys, Dad. Picture this." Campbell motioned with his hands. "A bat-shaped manta ray jumping out of the waves. An osprey soaring through the blue sky. It's the real Florida."

Campbell was in his element, relaxed and animated, the way the sea always made his feel. Rex realized now that he had been wrong to try and push Campbell into studying law.

"And just wait 'til you see a sunset on the west coast. The sun just melts into the sea."

"It all sounds amazing. That reminds me—I promised I'd call your grandmother when we were on our way. I should make sure Moira is all right."

Mrs. Graves assured Rex that Moira had arrived safely and was comfortably installed at Heather Sutherland's house. "Where are ye now?"

"We're headed down to the Keys."

"I hope you're not driving and talking on the phone at the same time!"

"Campbell's SUV is an automatic. It only requires one hand to drive, and we're on a straight road. Mother, I have another call coming in … I'll call you back." Rex pressed the incoming call button. "Helen! How are you, love?"

"Is this a good time?"

"It's a perfect time!"

"I got your messages. Sorry I didn't call sooner. I needed to think things through."

"Is everything okay between us?"

"Yes, and I realize I should have been more supportive."

"Och, you're a wonderful woman, d'you know that?"

A pause from Helen. "Is she back in Edinburgh?"

"Aye, I just spoke with my mother. Moira's doing fine. I had to promise to visit her, just to get her on the plane. I hope you know it means nothing."

"I do, and I shouldn't have doubted you. Did you get to the bottom of the boy's suicide?"

"It wasna a suicide, as it turned out. He was murdered by another student, possibly accidentally. The good news is a boy who was wrongfully accused of a crime relating to the murder is being re-enrolled at the university. And Campbell has found himself a new love interest." He smiled across at his son, who was rereading his text messages. "It's the deceased boy's sister."

"That's sweet. It must be a relief for the parents to find out their son didn't take his own life after all. That's a terrible burden for any parent to bear. So what are you doing now?"

"We set off early for Islamorada. The property manager has left the key under the mat at the cottage where we're staying and said she stocked the refrigerator, since we won't be getting in until late."

"Sounds like fun."

"Aye, we're both ready for some rest and recreation. It's been a long week."

"How's it going with Campbell?"

"Just grand. He was a great help in the case. The lad has talents I never knew he possessed."

"Just wait until you see me hook a big tarpon," Campbell interjected.

"He says he's going to hook a big tarpon."

"What's that?" Helen asked.

"It's one of those monstrous fish they have here in Florida. I'll get it stuffed and bring it home with me."

Helen laughed. "A picture will do. Make sure you take lots of photos."

"For once I remembered to bring a camera."

"Are you still coming down to Derby next weekend?"

"Come Hell or high water."

As he and Helen said their fond goodbyes, he passed the sign for Interstate 4.

"We're making good time," he told Campbell. "We could take a detour into the Everglades when we get to the Sawgrass Expressway and see if we can spot some alligators. What do you think?"

"Let's do it, Pops!"

"Pops?" Rex asked in surprise. Glancing round, he saw that Campbell was grinning at him.

Grinning back, he tuned into the rock station he had discovered on the way north and turned up the volume on a song by Tom Petty and the Heartbreakers. "I feel like singing," he said.

Campbell groaned dramatically and, slumping in his seat, covered his ears.

ABOUT THE AUTHOR

Born in Bloomington, Indiana, and now residing permanently in Florida, C.S. Challinor was educated in Scotland and England, and holds a joint honors degree in Latin and French from the University of Kent, Canterbury, as well as a diploma in Russian from the Pushkin Institute in Moscow. She has traveled extensively and enjoys discovering new territory for her novels.

Visit C.S. Challinor on the web at www.rexgraves.com

A sneak peek at the next Rex Graves Mystery,
Murder on the Moor

ONE

"IT'S A PIG IN a poke," the contractor decreed, shaking his head dubiously at the cast iron radiator in the guest bedroom of Rex's converted hunting lodge.

"Aye," agreed McCallum's equally stout younger brother. "Ye should hae switched to contemporary models," he told Rex, "like we said when ye first purchased this place. These old radiators retain more heat, but if this'un continues to leak, you'll end up wi' a rotten floorboard. The radiator is so corroded it could come off the wall and fall onto somebody's heed."

"I like these radiators," Rex protested. "They have character."

"Ye canna let emotion get in the way of good sense," the first Mc-Callum chided, looking at Rex as though he were a clueless twit and not a preeminent Scottish barrister. "Now, it can be fixed— if yer heart is set on it, but it will cost ye."

"Aye," seconded the brother. "Parts are dear. Not many of these radiators left around the country."

"Why can't you just solder the damn thing?"

With exaggerated patience, the elder McCallum launched into an ABC of plumbing basics.

"How long to fix it?" Rex finally asked. "I have guests arriving this afternoon."

"Och, it canna be done afore then," the elder McCallum exclaimed. "Ye'll have to keep the pan there to collect the water until we can get back sometime next week."

This was not reassuring, especially the "sometime next week" part. The local labor force adhered to the typical Highland attitude toward work: It would get done when desire for food or whisky absolutely drove them to the necessity of it, and not before.

"Now, take heed," the younger brother said. "The leak will likely get worse, so I suggest ye get a bigger pan."

"We'll take fifty pounds now for the consultation," the other said. "Ta verra much, squire," he added as he pocketed the money in greedy anticipation of an afternoon at the pub.

Rex was now anxious to get the two men out of the lodge before Helen returned from the village store and saw the mud they had tracked up the stairs on their work boots. She was as industrious and house-proud as a badger and had spent the past two days sprucing up the place in preparation for the housewarming party.

He felt less enthusiastic about the proceedings. The whole point of the lodge, after all, had been for them to spend time together by themselves. A stroke of luck had brought him to this property near Inverness, a few hours' drive north of Edinburgh, where he lived.

It might seem odd and slightly suspect to some people that a mature man would live at home with an aging, if still sprightly parent, but the arrangement had made sense when Rex lost his wife. He had not wanted Campbell, then fifteen, coming home from school to an empty house, and so he had moved back in with his mother.

Now that Campbell was away at college in Florida, Rex felt an increasing desire to spread his wings.

After mopping up the mess on the stairs, he wandered down the path to wait for Helen at the gate. The lodge stood sideways to the loch, which at first sight seemed odd, but in fact was quite logical. Logic always counted more for Rex than aesthetics and may have been the reason the Victorian hunting lodge had not been snapped up sooner.

The front door— at the side of the house— faced north toward the village of Gleneagle. The conservatory built onto the south side hoarded any sun the thrifty Highland summer deigned to bestow within its glass walls and looked upon a garden carpeted with bluebells and hedged by late-flowering rhododendrons and azaleas.

The best view, though, was reserved for the living room, whose large windows opened onto the loch. This is where the logic of the architect back in 1845 came into play, for Loch Lown comprised only a narrow body of water, not much wider than the breadth of the house, and by positioning the lodge in this perpendicular manner, the most important rooms embraced a long perspective of the lake.

Gleneagle Lodge was the only residence on the mile-long loch, which had once belonged to the laird of Gleneagle Castle, now a tattered ruin at the top of the hill in the direction of the village. Parcels of the estate had been successively sold off to honor the debts of the dissolute Fraser family, distant relations of the famous clan of that name, until the grounds had shrunk to the confines of the four-bedroom lodge, loch, and several hundred acres of hill and glen, currently in the proud possession of Rex Graves, Queen's Counsel.

The loch, though not large, was deep, and believed to connect by means of underwater tunnels via Loch Lochy, a neighboring lake, to

Loch Ness. Fortunately for Rex, Loch Lown was off the beaten path and sunk amid steep wooded hills surmountable only by one axle-breaking road or by the most energetic of hikers. Rex hoped his ubiquitous "Private Property—Keep Off" and "Deer Stalking Strictly Prohibited" signs would further deter the public from venturing onto his land.

He spotted a figure cresting the hill and, minutes later, the form of Helen appeared carrying a basket. He started out on the single-track road and began climbing. The hills around him bloomed with purple heather. The sunlight filtering between the pine trees warmed his shoulders. It would have been perfect weather were the air not rife with biting midges, the curse of Highland summers. Swatting them from his face, he smiled up at Helen as she plunged down the hill, her tweed skirt flopping above her knees, wisps of blond hair falling in her laughing blue eyes.

"I saw the McCallum van," she said as they met up on the road. "Did they fix the radiator?"

He would have gladly joined her on her walk to the village but for the appointment with the builders, which had been set for "sometime in the day."

"No, but they still managed to get a fifty out of me."

"Oh, Rex, you should have let me deal with them."

Helen was a practical woman and probably would not have put up with any nonsense from the McCallum brothers, but Rex felt it was a man's place to deal with loutish contractors.

"I suppose they drew sharp intakes of breath and heaved deep sighs of woe when they inspected the radiator," she added.

"Aye, pretty much."

"And they said it would cost an arm and a leg to fix anything so antiquated."

"They did, only they didn't express themselves in such eloquent terms." He took Helen's basket and they walked toward the lodge gate.

"I know how you feel about supporting the local economy, Rex, but I think they are taking advantage."

"Aye, but they're right clannish around here. If I hired a townie, I'd be shunned by the whole village. They'd put a hex on those eggs you bought."

Helen laughed outright. "You're just a big-hearted softie. I cannot imagine you sending people off to prison."

"It's my job."

"When are they coming back to fix it?"

"Next week," Rex said with a conviction he did not feel.

"Ah, well, at least no one will be using that room. It's only Alistair and the Farquharsons staying over, isn't it?"

Rex groaned at the thought. The Farquharsons were horrible snobs, but they had contributed ostentatiously to his mother's pet charity and she had insisted he put them up for a few days. Alistair was a colleague from the High Court of Justiciary, the supreme criminal court of Scotland, and had given him the tip about Gleneagle Lodge, having heard of the sale from a solicitor friend.

"Who else did you say was coming?" Helen asked.

"The Allerdice couple who own a hotel on Loch Lochy on the other side of Deer Glen. They're bringing their son and daughter. Donnie has a learning disability. The lass is a bit of a wallflower. The parents are anxious to marry her off."

Helen rolled her eyes. "How feudal."

"They asked if they could bring a guest from the hotel. He's writing an article on Lizzie, Loch Lochy's answer to Nessie of Loch Ness fame. I gather the plesiosaurs are cousins, or some such nonsense."

"Oh, I heard all about that at the village shop. Old Cameron spotted Lizzie this morning when he was fishing for pike. He said the creature fits the description of the Loch Ness monster, only it's smaller."

"It'll grow by the end of the night," Rex predicted. "That story will be worth a few drams at the pub."

"Isn't it exciting? A prehistoric monster living in the neighbouring loch!"

"Och, c'mon, now— it's a big hoax!"

They reached the side of the lodge, with its red gingerbread gable culminating in a generous chimney. The newly varnished oak door formed the only aperture in the gray stone wall. Flanked by two huge pots of geraniums, it displayed a brass knocker and a plaque engraved with "R. Graves" above the letter box, leaving no doubt as to the main entry to the house. Previously, visitors had wandered about in some confusion, peering into downstairs windows, much to Rex's annoyance.

"Well, I best get on with my cake," Helen said. "What time will they be arriving?"

"Around six." Rex wondered if he should change out of his corduroys, and decided he couldn't be bothered. "Can I do anything to help?"

"It's all taken care of, except for the smoked salmon canapés. But you can keep me company in the kitchen if you want."

"I'd rather keep you company somewhere else," Rex growled. "I do wish these people weren't coming."

"Oh, come on, Rex. It'll be *fun*."

At that moment, he heard the rumble of an engine on the other side of the hill and seconds later saw a Land Rover hurtling down the incline. An arm shot out of the passenger window waving a

205

bright scarf, followed by a middle-aged aristocratic face framed by beige, shoulder length hair.

"Well, he-llo!" Mrs. Farquharson bleated. "We found you!"

Worst luck, Rex thought.

The next moment he was introducing Estelle and Cuthbert Farquharson to Helen.

"*Ceud mile failte*," Helen welcomed them. "I've been practicing my Scots Gaelic."

Cuthbert babbled some incomprehensible Gaelic politeness in reply before turning to Rex. "I say, I thought we'd get in a bit of deer stalking." He clapped Rex on the back. "Plenty of time before dinner, what?"

Cuthbert Farquharson sported a Sherlock Holmes deerstalker and matching camouflage trousers bagging over sage green rubber boots. Estelle also wore Wellies, along with a sloppy sweater and frumpy tweed skirt, the attire of landed gentry. Though Scottish, they had both been educated in England, Estelle at some highfaluting London school and Cuthbert at Eton, which accounted for their horsy accents.

"How bloody marvelous this place is," Estelle remarked prior to inhaling deeply of the fresh air. "So wild and unspoilt." She cast a determined look at the lodge, apparently undaunted by the idea of "slumming it" and prepared for any eventuality. "Doesn't look like anything's changed much over the centuries. It's so *authentic!*"

"We do have indoor plumbing," Rex countered mildly. "In fact, all modern conveniences." Then, remembering the leaking radiator, he added, "Of sorts."

"Your room is all ready for you," Helen told the guests. "I was just about to bake a cake."

"A cake! How fabulous!" Estelle enthused.

"With real eggs, fresh from the local farm," Rex added with a straight face.

"Divine. Do let me help."

"Good idea." Cuthbert prodded his wife in Helen's direction. "The ghillie should be here in a minute with the pony," he told Rex.

"What ghillie?"

"The boy from the Loch Lochy Hotel. His parents and sister will be along later with that reporter chap."

"We won't be needing a ghillie or a pony," Rex said firmly. "We won't be shooting any deer."

Ponies were still the transportation of choice for retrieving dead deer over hilly terrain.

"But I brought my new rifle. Thought I'd try it out."

"The only thing we shoot here are photographs," Rex explained.

A deer head replete with a pair of seven-pointed antlers had hung over the living room fireplace when he purchased the lodge. The first thing he had done was to give it a decent burial and replace it with a copy of Monarch of the Glen, the famous oil painting of a majestic stag by nineteenth-century artist Sir Edwin Landseer.

"Did you bring a camera?" he asked his guest.

"Estelle has a Nikon somewhere." Cuthbert's bottom lip, red and wet as a woman's, trembled peevishly. "Not quite the same thing, is it?"

"I don't believe in murdering God's creatures for sport."

"You can't view them as defenseless bambies, you know. They wreak havoc with the forests. Without wolves to cull the population, it's the best way to keep the numbers under control."

Rex shook his head resolutely. "Not on my land. I like to think of Gleaneagle Lodge as a nature sanctuary."

At that moment, a golden eagle swooped overhead and soared over the hill.

"Well, it's your land, I suppose, and you're free to do with it as you please," Cuthbert conceded. "Here's the boy now."

An uneven clopping of hooves rang out as Donnie Allerdice, an agile lad of about seventeen in a plaid shirt and jeans, led a sturdy Shetland pony down the loose stone road.

"This here is Honey," he told the men when he drew level with them. "On account of the colour of her coat, not her temperament." He said this in a slow and deliberate way. The horse chewed irritably on its bit and twitched its long tail. "The midges are bothering her something fierce."

"You can put her in the meadow over there for the time being," Rex told the boy, who was slightly cross-eyed. "We won't be needing her."

"Mr. Graves is opposed to hunting," Cuthbert explained testily.

"That's a shame," the boy said. "I saw a large hummel and his hinds down in the glen." Rex noticed he carried a sheath knife in his belt.

"A hummel, eh?" Cuthbert questioned. "Those are pretty rare. They don't grow antlers," he told Rex. "I wouldn't mind taking a look. Could you show me?" he asked the boy.

Rex reached out for the rifle. "Before you go, could you leave this? I'll put it in the house."

Cuthbert reluctantly handed it over. A military-looking telescopic lens was mounted on the gun. Rex reflected that a deer would never stand a chance against such a state-of-the-art example of ruthless weaponry.

He had better put it somewhere safe.